Nathaniel

BLOOD BROTHERHOOD BOOK 6

KATHI S. BARTON

This is a work of fiction. Names, characters, places, and incidents are products of the author's imagination or are used fictitiously and are not to be construed as real. Any resemblance to actual events, locations, organizations, or persons, living or dead, is entirely coincidental.

World Castle Publishing, LLC
Pensacola, Florida
Copyright © Kathi S. Barton 2016
Paperback ISBN: 9781629896113
eBook ISBN: 9781629896120
First Edition World Castle Publishing, LLC, December 26, 2016
http://www.worldcastlepublishing.com

Licensing Notes

Cover: Karen Fuller
Editor: Maxine Bringenberg

Chapter 1

The motor home coughed a couple times but continued down the road. Looking in the rearview mirror, she wondered what she'd been thinking picking something so fucking big to use to get away. The thing was top of the line, sure, but for just her, it was too much. Simply too much of everything. She had to smile while pulling into the gas station. It felt like she was filling this sucker up every ten minutes.

"I'm certainly doing my part in stimulating the economy by using this." The lines were short, so she pulled into the bay closest to the road. Stretching her neck before getting out, she felt a stab of pain in her heart and sat very still to see where it went next. When she felt nothing more, she stood up and made her way to the pumps.

Beth knew that should her heart shut down while she was driving, she might hurt someone else when she crashed. It was why she was very careful and took precautions that were well beyond what older people did when informed they had a defective ticker. And she had one as faulty as possible. She'd been dealt a bad hand, as her grandma used to say.

Beth Snow was going to die because of her heart. Not because it was broken, which in a way it was, but because it was enlarged...too big to function properly. It would come much sooner than anyone could have guessed, especially her and her family, but it was a fact and she wanted it to happen on her terms. It was the reason for this trip. The lie behind going to see some sites before she settled down.

Beth wanted to be as far from her parents as she could when the time came. She knew her mom would be…her mom and dad would be devastated. He still will be either way, but she didn't want him there when it occurred. That wasn't right either. She wanted them both there, but was trying to spare them the pain of it.

It's not that they were mean to her. No, never that. But they did have a way about them that would bring out the worst in each other. Her mother was controlling, manipulative, as well as whiney, and had been since Beth was little. She didn't like when things weren't going her way, and she did something about it, even to the point of being rude and nasty.

Her mom, Ruth, would get something in her head, or she'd want someone to do things her way. Then when they disagreed or didn't meet her expectations, she'd do it herself. That never went over well in their neighborhood, and it had caused some horrible fights, with the police being called in and her dad having to pay some fine, bail her mom out, then apologize to whoever it was she had upset.

Even her dad wasn't immune to her mom's manipulative behavior, and when he didn't do something or say the right thing to her, she would want Beth to call and make him do whatever it was that week. Like that was ever going to happen. Beth was the daughter, not her babysitter, and certainly not her dad's task master.

Her dad, Lyle, was a quiet man. He had worked hard for the money that Mom spent to keep up with the neighbors. And even though retired some years ago, they didn't want for anything and had made sure that as their only child she didn't either. But as soon as she'd turned eighteen, she'd gone out in the world on her own and made herself as independent as possible. She had made a good living at it as well by following in her dad's footsteps and becoming an engineer. But leaving them like she had, that was the smartest thing she'd ever done, she thought. For a lot of reasons. The last face to face conversation with her mom had sealed that deal.

"I don't understand how you think this is going to make you get any better. Just let us go with you and keep you on the right track to getting well. It's not like we have anything to do. Your father hasn't worked in several years." Beth could have pointed out that he'd retired from his job but still had a very good income. And when they wanted something, he'd go find something fun to do to pay for it and not touch their savings. She looked at her dad and could see while he was hurt too, he sort of understood because this was, after all, her mom. "Tell her, Lyle. Tell her that she needs to let us go with her so she can get better. We can't make sure that she's doing what it takes for her to get well if we're not there."

"Ruth, I think she's right." Her mom turned her back to him, and Beth knew that later she'd tell her dad how he was wrong to have said those things and that he should have agreed with her. "This will be good for her. Kinda wish I'd taken a trip like this when I was younger. See a little of this big world before things get all hinky. But she needs this and I think she's doing what she needs to. Not just for her, either."

Hinky. What a wonderful word to say his little girl was going to die. "I'll send you postcards and when I can, I'll call you once a week. I really do need this."

"Well, I hope you know that you're both wrong in this. I can't make sure that you're eating properly or taking care of yourself if you won't allow me this. Bethany, you know as well as I do that you're going to need me to make sure that you're doing all the right things to get well." Her mother put her hand on her arm and hugged her. "You need me now as much as you did when you were a little girl and had the flu. Just tell us where you're going and we'll travel along with you. There's a good girl."

"Mom, I'm not going to get well. I'm going to die. And soon. You know this. The doctor told us that there is nothing he can do for me. Not even a transplant is going to help me now. It's too late for me."

Beth wanted to take the words back but her mom slapped her, something that she'd never done in all her life. Without another word, her mom turned her back on her too and went into the house. Beth was sure that, even though she was upset with her, her mom had gone in and started packing her things to go anyway.

"Go, baby. Go now before she comes out here and loads her things up in that home of yours while we stand here, and is aghast that she's ready before you are." Beth hugged her father, knowing deep inside her heart that it would be the last for them both. "I love you, baby girl. I have loved you since the moment you took your first breath, and will well after you take your last. Be careful and have fun."

When he let go, he left her too. She'd seen the tears then, streaming down his face, and had gotten into her moving home and left. That had been six months ago. According to her doctor, Beth had only one or two of the six to eight months he'd given her to live left.

The gas pump popped, signaling that it was finished, startled her from her thoughts. Putting the handle back in the little slot, she looked around while the receipt printed. She would have to find a place to rest soon, a campground that would take her big rig, and settle in for a few days. She might even go see some of the sights while here, she thought, and got into the camper. Starting the engine, she let her broken heart mend a little as she made her way back into the traffic.

The campground was quiet this time of year. She supposed that most vacationers would've had their fill of camping by now. Late winter was not really a go to a place in a motor home kind of time. Smiling to herself, she watched as snow started to fall while fixing herself some soup and then settled down to enjoy it. Beth didn't bother with the television, and if asked, she did not even know if she could turn it on. It was the quiet that she wanted.

The books that she'd picked up here and there were on the shelves that didn't have souvenirs on them. A pretty stone that she'd gotten in a national park. A pinecone she'd picked up at a roadside picnic area that she just couldn't resist. All of these things and the rest were all labeled and dated. When someone came to get her home someday, she knew that her dad would enjoy these bits of her trip. And the pictures on her computer were in files as well. She'd been sending him emails with them attached when she had service.

Beth was pragmatic about things. She was going to die, that was a done deal. But she wasn't going to wallow in self-pity, nor was she going to roll over and let it take her. She was going out doing the things that she wanted. Just the way her dad had taught her to be. Happy to the end.

It was nearly nine when she decided to call home. If her mom answered she'd never get to speak to her dad, and Beth was disappointed when she picked up the phone. After telling her several times that yes, she was taking her medicine, and she was resting and eating well, her mom started in on where she was and how they could meet her there.

"We bought a camper like yours the other day. It's very beautiful. The same color and everything. It'll be hard to tell us apart when we're in the campgrounds together." Beth felt her belly churn up. "Your father thought it was a bad idea, but I told him that if you needed us, we should be prepared. So we're ready for you to tell us where you are so we can join you. Of course, you'll have to wait for us. It would be silly for you to go on and us not be with you, after all the trouble we've gone to."

"Mom, why did you make Dad buy a motor home when I told you that I wanted to do this on my own?" Her mom said she'd done no such thing. "You said he didn't want to but you told him to. Sounds to me like you made him."

"Well, if you're going to be nasty about it, Bethany, perhaps you should just come on home and we can settle this here and not by shouting at each other on the phone." She told her that she wasn't coming home. "I think that's a wonderful idea, now that you mention it. I nearly forgot that it was Christmas in a few weeks. Either come home, so we can be together as a family, or we go there. It's up to you, dear. It's not that difficult to give me directions, is it? I'll have your father map them out too, just to make sure we can get there in a reasonable time. You know how he is. But I'm thinking that if you come back here, that would be wonderful too. You've been gone for so long. Also, I tried to get your things out of storage but the man in charge said no. He even called the police on me, if you can believe that. You'll have to tell him that it's all right for me to get in there. That way, when you get back here, everything will be just how you want it."

"No. I don't want you bothering my things. I'm not coming back there, and for sure you are not going to come here. I know how you are, as does Dad. Mom, I'm not going to let you know where I am, nor am I going to do whatever else you have on that list in your head that no one messes with. I'm going to do this on my own, in my own way." Her mother laughed then, that twittering sort of laughter that made her think she was humoring her. "Mom, can I speak to Dad? Please?"

"He's busy tinkering with the motor home. I told him that he should just let someone who knows what they're doing mess with things, but he gets something in his head and he won't stop until I have to make him." Beth heard some paper moving around. "Now, I have a map and paper right here. Tell me what state you're in and I can figure out from there how we can—"

"Mom, Dad is an engineer. I'm pretty sure that he could do a better tinkering job than most of the people who actually built that thing." Her mom huffed. "I'd very much like to speak to Dad. I want to find out what you did to make him do this for you."

"What a thing to say to your own mother. You make it sound as if I stand over him with a whip and order him about." Beth said she did. "I don't know what you're on right now, but you'll not talk to me that way, Bethany. I am your mother. And don't think I've not noticed that I don't have that address yet."

"I know that you're my mom. And he's my dad. Now put him on the phone or I'll hang up and you'll not know what the doctor said to me." There wasn't any doctor, and she had no different news than she'd had six months ago. But her mother lived on having as much information as possible on her illness, as she called it, so she could tell all her friends. Beth was sure that every person in any place her mother went knew as much about her heart condition as her own doctor

11

did. "Mom?"

"I don't think you're being very civil to me, Bethany. And as soon as we get there, I'm going to make sure you realize how badly you hurt me. If you want to talk to your father, then fine. There is no reason for you to get snippy with me." She heard the phone slam down on something hard and smiled.

Beth was sure that, even though they had a cordless phone in every part of the house, her mom never went beyond the five or so feet from the base that as she'd done when there had been corded phones in the house. And Beth would bet all her money that it would never have occurred to her to take the cordless to her father so that she could speak to him. Then when they were finished using the phone, no matter where they were when that occurred, she would put it right back in the cradle like she always had before.

"Hello, baby girl. How is life treating you?" And just like that, the weight of the world was lifted off her shoulders. When she started crying, she heard him speaking again. "Oh honey, don't cry. I'm here for you. And if you give me just a minute, I'll talk to you in my office."

She heard her mom telling him not to be stupid, that she would like to hear the lies he was telling their daughter and to stay right where she could hear him. Mom even told him that if he did go into his office, he'd better not shut the door. Beth smiled when she heard it shut and the lock turn.

"Dad, she's going to be really pissed at you when you get back out there." He only laughed and asked her what was going on. "Nothing. I just heard that Mom made you buy a camper. I'm so sorry."

"Don't be. If things keep going like this, I might just start living out there in it. It's a nice sucker. Have you worked out how the extensions come out yet? I swear to you, things get more and more complicated than they need to be." She'd forgotten to extend the sides again. Not that it mattered…she had more than enough room. "I got the propane tanks filled today. Then I got a few groceries to stash in it, though I didn't tell your mother. The fridge is all hooked up and cold. I even installed some solar panels on the top of it so the batteries can be charged when we're not using them. I'm betting you haven't even turned on the telly, nor have you used that impressive stove that it has either, have you, darling?"

"No to all of it. But I did notice that I have one, if that makes a difference. And the microwave has been wonderful for my many flavors of soup, too. But if I were you, Dad, I'd do that. You should just get up one morning while she's in bed and take a trip. Maybe not return." He told her that he'd think on that. "I miss you, Daddy."

"And I you. Are you feeling all right? Taking care, aren't you?" She told him she was, just tired a lot more. "Yes, that's what they told us would happen. You just take it easy. Oh, before I forget, I got a cell phone today. I'll give you the number to call me directly. I put it on vibrate so she doesn't know about it, but I wanted to be able to talk when you wanted."

After she wrote down the number, they talked for another twenty minutes. By the time she closed off the connection, Beth was exhausted. As she was getting into bed, she realized that not once did he say that he wasn't going to take off, nor did he ask her where she was. Beth loved her parents, but her dad was her world.

~~~

Remy looked at the sky and saw nothing out of the ordinary. Every day he expected Benton to come to them, show himself off, but nothing as yet. It had been nearly two weeks since the earth had let them know he'd risen, and in that time, none of them had dropped their guard. He looked over when he heard the clash of swords, and saw that it was a near war between Nate and Skylar.

Both of them had come a long way in working out their differences. Mostly he thought it was due to Rick making the man come out of his shell, but Nate now joined in on more activities, and had just started to have meals with them. He ate a great deal all the time because of what was done to him in the other realm, but was getting that under control as well.

Whey, his own little faerie, as he'd told Remy, landed on his shoulder, and Remy asked him if things were going well.

"Yes, my lord. And thank you ever so much for the greenhouse. It has cooled tempers a great deal to have something to keep busy with." He told him that it had been Ryiah's idea and Whey nodded. "I have a request, my lord. We should like to plan a party when the spring comes. We have not had one for a very long time, and I think it would be a good thing."

"Spring is several months away. You think you need that much time for me to approve it now?" He told him that he did. That flowers had to be ready for such an event. "I see. Well, yes, a party would be great. I was wondering about the tree. Have you found some decorations for the big one that's going up?"

"We have. Oh, so many that will grace the tree. Some of the fireflies have said they'd be our lights on it, and that will be a wonderful sight as well." Remy tensed up when he saw Skylar hit the ground. "She is well, my lord. The earth, it takes good care of her should she fall again. See, even now it helps her rise up. She will never be harmed in this play."

"I think she falls just to get me to run to her aid. What do you think?" Of course Whey disagreed with him, saying that

Skylar wasn't that mean. But when she turned and winked at them both, Remy laughed. "I think we've been had, Whey. My lovely mate is playing with our emotions."

"Women do that well, I think. My own bride, she is making me silly with her ways. Did I mention that the queen has picked us to work with the newborns when it is time for them to be born?" Remy nodded. He'd been told that at least twenty times an hour for the last several days. "She finally put up the list. Margo and I will be working with the roses. It's such an honor."

Remy had learned a great deal about flowers and faeries. First of all, not every bloom was filled with one of the tiny babes. The flower had to be kissed by a faerie that the queen had chosen. And while many worked for her, only a select few could give the flowers the babes that would eventually work for her too. Also, and this one was a shock to him as well, brownies were the babies that were forgotten or missed. Some of them would fall into the earth when the flower opened, but a great many of them would take wings as soon as the sun opened the blooms and find themselves a place to work with and for children. This was where imaginary friends came from. The brownies would live with the children until they no longer needed them. Remy still wondered if a child born of this current world would ever not need them.

"I meant to ask you, when the brownies are no longer needed by the children, what do they do? I mean, they're still around, correct?" Whey assured him that they were. "But where do they go?"

"To live with the elders of your kind. There are a great many of them—the elders, I mean—that have no one but the brownies that come to visit. Some stay until they pass on, others visit and talk with a few at a time. The brownies serve a great function in your world that humans at a certain age never know about." Remy thought that was the nicest thing he'd heard in a long while, and told his friend that. "Thank you, my lord. Should you see one, an elder, watch how they smile for no reason. It is the brownie telling them a story so that they will not be sad."

Remy decided that he'd make sure to thank the queen for such a service to the humans, both young and old. As they made their way to the couple still at play, Remy decided that he'd very much like to have a few of the little people come and live with him and Skylar. When they were finished with the war, he wanted to settle down and have a houseful of them around. Mostly to talk to—they were extremely intelligent—but also because they made him feel good. Not just physically, but also mentally.

"I've something to show you when you have a moment." Remy told Nate that now was a good time. "It's my tat. The one I was telling you about. We're to have company. And I'm not sure what to do about it."

"What do you mean? Benton? He's coming?" Nate shook his head and pulled his shirt over his head and turned. The tat was moving, and Remy was nearly sick with it. When it settled, he didn't see much until Skylar pointed out that there were twelve now, not eleven on his back. "Your mate is coming? Is that what you're telling me? Good job, Nate. You'll be happy as—"

"No, a woman is coming. Just because every other female that has come here has turned out to be someone's mate, doesn't mean that she's for me. I don't know what I'd do with a mate." When he started to ask again what he meant, Skylar put her hand on his arm. She told him to wait. "I've things to do, so I thank you, Skylar, for the lesson."

When he was gone, Remy looked at Skylar for an explanation. "He is so large, have you noticed that? And with his size comes certain things that frighten him."

It took him a moment to understand. His size would frighten most men, he thought. Then he thought of all the things that might make a mate be fearful.

"He thinks he'd harm her during sex." Even though it wasn't a question, she told him that was it. "I don't see him hurting her. Whatever has happened to him, he won't harm her. He must know that it's not possible should he even think he would."

"He's aware of that. He won't want to harm her, but he's terrified that he will. He's fearful of crushing her." It took Remy a minute to get what she meant and his face heated. "Even after all the ways you have taken me, against any hard surface you can put me on, you still get embarrassed when I talk about sex with you? Remy, you're a child at heart, I think."

"I'm a man that isn't used to such talk from someone. While you and I have a healthy relationship, I try my best not to think of the rest of them having it. Aye, I know that they do, like rabbits, but I don't think about the physical aspect of it."

When she giggled he smiled at her. "You're such an old man. I think that's what I love about you. How you can be so prudish one minute and like a sexed crazed animal the next." She wrapped her arms around him and he held her to his body. She looked at his shoulder and he only just remembered they had company.

"Whey, 'tis time you found your own mate."

The little faerie laughed and said he would do just that. When he was gone, Remy lifted his mate into his arms and took her to their room. It was time to show his little woman just how sexed crazed he really was.

"I love you, Rembrandt. With all that I am." He kissed her then and felt his heart fill with her words. "When you touch me like this, even when you need it as much as I do, I can't think of a single reason for us to be apart. I need you as much as I do air in my lungs."

Remy thought himself the luckiest man in the world. And when she kissed him, he felt his heart fill once again with her love and nearly wept with his need for her. Before he took her to bed, he pulled back from her just far enough to get her attention. He needed her to understand something that he'd been thinking about for days now.

"I should like to have many children with you. Not to replace the ones I lost, but to have our love bonded in a way I never had with my first mate. She was everything to me, don't get me wrong, but you are so much more. Watching you grow with a child of ours? You cannot know what that thought does for me." He kissed her again and watched her face.

"Remy, I swear to you that sometimes the words that come from your mouth are enough to melt even the coldest of hearts." He grinned at her. "Yes, having children with you, watching you play and hold them, is all I think about when I'm alone. When I see you with the other children in the compound, I want to have you fill me with one of our own. To have a son or daughter would fulfill me in ways that I never thought possible, so long as you are there beside me to help nurture and love them."

"And I shall be, my love. For the rest of our lives." He lifted her chin up to see her beautiful face. "We have avoided the conversation that has been haunting us for days now. Would you like to discuss it now?"

"No. Not yet. I know what I want to do in my head, but

not in my heart just yet." He understood that. It was the same for him. "After. I want to talk about it after."

"All right."

Taking her to their bed, he stripped her down to bare skin. Each part of her, every inch of her, was marked by some unknown magic. Kissing her now, he knew that someday they'd know what they were here for, why something had chosen them for this task. But for now, at this moment, he wanted to make love to his mate. Remy knew they had plenty of time to talk about the other.

Sliding his cock deep into her, he grinned when she screamed out the first of what he knew was going to be many releases. He too would enjoy her. For now, they were just a normal couple having an afternoon of fun.

Chapter 2

Nate felt the tat move again and got up to see it. Every hour for the last few days he'd known that it was changing. Today it had moved more than ever before, and he had a feeling that it was because whoever she was, she was getting close.

He'd never been in love before. He had liked women, still did...very much so. But since this thing with Benton and the drugs that had been put in him when he was in the other realm, Nate tried his best not to think of them. But of course when he tried that, it was all he thought about.

He'd lost so much in all of this. He thought more than the rest, but wasn't sure they'd see it that way. His life had been at an end. Not because he'd been dying like the rest of them had, but because he'd been about to take his own life. Even Chris, a dragon of all things, hadn't been ill, but he'd been changed and seemed all right with it. Not Nate.

He no longer hated Hector for doing this to him. Nate didn't care much for him, but he didn't hate him. As Vicki had pointed out, it was a waste of time and energy. But that didn't mean he had to like the turn of events. Nate looked in the mirror again when he felt the shift.

Whoever this woman was, she was ill. He had no idea how he knew that, but it was something that had occurred to him when he'd woke this morning. And when she came here, and it looked as if she was, then Benton was going to kill her. That was something else he would have shared with Remy had they been alone. It was a conversation that he hated to bring to light, but he wanted Remy to know as well as the others. They needed to be ready for him.

Benton was stronger. Not only had his body taken on more energy, but it had healed as well. His scales were now whole, and his tail, along with his arm, had come back. He wasn't sure what had done that, but Nate thought it had to do with the water he'd been in. Something about it had reacted with the drugs in his system. Nate was terrified that he'd fall into the water and change as well. That would be all he needed, to grow bigger than he was now.

"Into what, I wonder." He was already a monster, in his opinion. He was sure that things could get worse for him, but he was willing to bet not too much more. As he watched his back, the tat changed again and he saw her standing beside a road, a motor home just behind her.

He'd not had this sort of view of her before. All the others, the brotherhood and their mates, were there, but in a circle around her. Their faces were turned to her, as if watching while they were framed around her. He noticed too that he wasn't in the frame with all the others, but watched as another motor home pulled up beside hers. For whatever reason, Nate thought she was in trouble and felt the need to go to her aid.

Moving to his door and pulling his shirt back on as he went, Nate wondered where he'd say he was going when asked. For sure he knew it was along the highway, but other than that, he had not a single clue. Moving toward the underground garage, he saw Chris and paused when he asked him where he was going.

"If I tell you, will you try and not freak out on me?"

Chris grinned at him and crossed his arms over his chest. "I'm a person that teaches fifth graders, in a so different part of the world than we're in now that it boggles my mind, how to understand and write English. For the most part I'm a man, but I can change into any animal I want when I need to. And if the shit has really hit the fan, I can blend my animal with Kate's and we become giant and deadly. I think getting freaked out is never going to happen." Nate turned and pulled his shirt off again. "Okay, I was wrong. Does that fucking move when you need it to?"

"I don't have any idea. But she needs me." Chris nodded and asked if he could come along. "Are you in the frame?"

Chris looked. "No. I was going to say yes, just beside Kate and Remy, but I'm gone now. Does that mean I'm dead or going with you?" Chris got in the truck that Nate had been using and closed the door as he reached for his seatbelt. "This girl, she's your mate, right? I'm assuming that's why you have to go and save her."

"I haven't any idea." Chris said nothing and Nate felt bad for lying to him. "Okay, I might have an idea, but that doesn't mean I'm going to act on this. Have you seen how fucking huge I am? I'd kill her the first time I gave her a hug."

"So? Be gentle when you hug her, try your best to hold yourself back a little. You can do it. And I'm sure you're not just talking about hugs. Sex can be pretty intense, sure, but you'd just be gentle with her. It's in your blood, or some shit like that." Nate reminded him that his blood had been fucked with. "Yeah, there is that, but you'll still be easy with her because you just know that you have to be."

Nate didn't say anything. He wasn't really sure what to say to him. He'd just know to be gentle? How the hell did that even work during sex? When he was making love to a woman, he rarely thought of anything but her pleasure, not how hard he was fucking her. As he pulled onto the highway, Chris asked him where they were going.

"I know that she's here somewhere and close. But other than that, I have no idea. I also know that she's driving a large motor home and that someone pulled up beside her. The feeling of fear and pain was just there. I don't know why." Chris nodded. "I have to tell you something that I've only shared with Rick. I know that at some point in this, Benton kills her. It's different every time it happens, but he kills her. I don't know what to do about it, because I haven't any idea how to stop him."

Nate expected Chris to tell him not to let it happen, but he only sat there. When Nate was sure he was being ignored, Chris leaned back on the seat and looked at him. Like really looked at him.

"Rick said that the events leading up to her getting killed are different." He asked Chris when he'd spoken to him. "Just now. They saw us leaving, and since no one knows how to talk to you yet through a link, they asked me where we were headed. I told him what was going on so that no one would come after us. So this thing, this dream…it changes all the time? But the end is the same, correct?"

"Yes, the events change, like at what point it occurs and where she is when it happens, but not her death. He tears her in half each time. At one point we were all dead when he did it. But that's since changed. As we got stronger, I guess, we were killed at different times. Like some of us before she is killed, then the rest after. Or after he kills her, then the rest of us die." He asked him if he could see it on his back or was it just a dream. "No. Today is the first time that I could only see a single person, and there has been...I guess you could call it movement all day. And yes, I can feel when the tat changes. Usually we're all there, not the woman, but the rest of us. The part that I know about her being killed, that's in my dreams I have about her and the rest of us."

"And even though the events change, the outcome is the same? We all die."

Nate nodded as he passed some vehicles. It was strange seeing them being driven. It had been a long while since there had been enough humans around to even consider getting the cars up and running. They'd have to figure out how to get the gas pumps going at the stations. As it was now, they were lucky that their cars and trucks at the compound were always full.

They knew that beyond their compound, several thousand miles as a matter of fact, things were going on as if nothing had come from another realm. Hector thought it was because of the proximity to the mountains and stones — agates — here, but no one knew for sure.

The stones had a great deal of value to other realms. While he'd never really put much thought into such an ordinary stone, he supposed that like most things, one person's trash was another's treasure. And here, the stones had been used to make more of the secondary, as well as third generation, monsters.

But for now they were keeping the monsters contained, what little there were of them. Less than a hundred by now he'd bet. And as soon as they dealt with Benton, then things would hopefully return to normal. Whatever the fuck that was.

As soon as he saw the motor home, he knew it was her. Getting off at the next exit, he got back on the highway going in the direction she'd been taking and pulled up behind her. He sat there for several seconds, trying to think what he was going to say to her, when Chris told him the second home was coming down the road, only about fifty miles back. Getting out, he made his way to the beautiful woman standing on the side of the road crying. Nate had to fight hard with himself not to take her into his arms and tell her that he'd make it right.

~~~

The flashy new truck didn't go by as the other vehicles had, but pulled up behind her. Beth wasn't sure what to do when the man got out and came toward her from the berm side. Run back into the camper and hope he didn't try to break in? Or did she stand here and let him murder her? When she saw the second man, she felt her fears not just double, but make her sick as well. The first man grinned at her, and she had a sudden urge to hit him. And that was so unlike her that she took a step back.

"I don't have any money on me. Nor do I have any credit cards. Not that you could use them until I get the bill. That's when I pay them.... I babble when I'm scared. And so you know, you're both scaring the shit out of me." Neither of them moved, and she realized that she was holding the tire iron in her hands. "I won't hurt you if you don't come any closer, all right?"

"We wanted to see if we could help you out. I can see that you're broken down." Beth glanced at the motor home, then back at the man who had gotten out on the driver's side. How the hell did they see that? "I can smell that it's overheated, and the smoke coming from the engine tells me that you might need a little water in the radiator. If that's not it, we can call someone to come and help you out. But I'm betting that's all

26

it is. Some water issues."

The second man went back to the truck and came back with two large water containers. She had no idea if they'd done something to her home to make it break down or not, but they were staying away from her. As he opened the hood to the home, she watched the first man as he stood staring at her.

"We won't hurt you. I swear, we're only here to help you out of a hinky situation." Her dad said that, hinky. He said it all the time, and she was pretty sure he didn't know he said it that much, just as this man didn't. No matter how bad the situation was or if there was more than likely a perfectly good name for it, it was only hinky to him. "If you want to go inside and lock the door, we'll fix it up and get you on your way. You won't have to come out until we're gone."

"How do I know you won't try and sabotage my home and leave me here for your partners in crime?" He laughed at her and she lifted the iron up higher. "I think that you should be on your way. I can call someone to come and help me. And for the record, I'm not as helpless as you think I am."

He moved. Beth wasn't sure how he'd cleared the distance between her and where he'd been, but he had her wrapped up in his arms and further off the road before she could blink. And when the large truck, not theirs, came off the road where she'd been standing and rolled over the embankment, Beth held onto the man tightly as she watched it land hard no more than a few feet from where they were. Then a man came staggering out of his now smoking car, holding his bloody head.

He would have hit her, and she was sure had she still been standing where she'd been, he'd have killed her. Not that she wasn't already close to dying, but she didn't want to go just yet. At least not like that anyway. Beth felt her knees go weak with fear, and the man lifted her up in his arms. She was in her camper holding a glass of water in seconds.

"I should go and check on him. He was bleeding. He might have.... His truck, it almost...." Beth held tightly onto the glass. "You saved my life."

"My friend, Chris, he's helping the man." She nodded and drank the water then set the glass down slowly. Her hands were shaking so badly she was surprised that she'd been able to hold the glass at all. "You're still very pale and I'm worried about you. Do you have anything stronger in here?"

"No. I can't drink alcohol with the meds I'm taking." He nodded and sat down across from her at the table. "You saved my life. Or you want me to think you did? Did you plan this to get in here?"

"No, I had nothing to do with him wrecking his vehicle. I heard the car coming and knew that he'd lost control at some point by the sound of his brakes. Getting you out of the way was all I could think of." She nodded. "You're not very trusting, are you?"

"Not really." She looked at him then. "You're very big, aren't you? I mean, like freaky big. Good looking, but.... I'm sorry, that was rude of me. I'm a little shaken. You said that the other man's name was Chris? Why do I think...? Never mind. I'm still a little freaked out."

"You're fine. I am big. And you're very small." She nodded. It was the meds; they had made her lose what little appetite she'd had. "I noticed all the pill bottles in the cabinet when I got you a glass. Are you unwell?"

"Unwell? No. I'm dying." He just nodded again, and she stood up but was shaking hard and had to sit again. "I hate to give you more reason to know that you can hurt me, but could you get me a glass of juice and my pills? I have to take them when my heart is pounding like this."

Instead of getting up, he put his hands over hers. They were warm and large, and Beth couldn't think why she'd not jerked hers away from him. But the longer he held her hands, the calmer her heart was. When she felt stronger and a little less lightheaded, she thanked him.

"My pleasure." The door opened behind him, and he didn't bother turning but spoke to the other man. "Is he all right? Did you call the police?"

"I did. He's drunk, like you said." Beth looked at both men. He'd known the other driver was drunk? And when had they spoken about that? "There is the other matter that we talked about. There's another home pulling up behind your truck now."

"Do you know who it might be? Or is it someone else that you thought could take me?" The first man only shrugged. But he did smile, and Beth felt...well, she wanted to think she was losing her mind, but she felt comforted by it this time. She looked at him. "What the hell are you two doing here?"

"My name is Nathaniel Livingston. Everyone calls me Nate. This is Chris Alexander." She pointed out to him that he hadn't answered her question. "No, but I'm trying to be polite by giving you our names so you'll not be so confused."

"I don't think that having your name is going to make me less confused. Who is in the second motor home?" Before either of them could reply, she heard her. Her mother was standing outside her door trying to open it, and screaming at the top of her lungs at Beth's dad. Beth asked him if he locked the door and Chris just nodded and grinned again. Beth looked at Nate. "Did you call her?"

"I don't even know who she is, so no, I didn't call her.

But there is a man with her, and he's not very happy." Before she could get that cleared up, her mom started pounding on the door again and yelling at her to open up. When she heard her father's voice, telling her mom to quiet down, the argument began. Or more than likely, a continuation of the same argument that they'd been having her entire life.

"I wasn't being loud, Lyle. But if she's sleeping, then I want her to hear me. The things you can get upset about. She's here; there is a car in the ditch and another one behind her. For all we know they could have gotten her pulled over in a ruse and are all now raping her." Beth watched Nate to see how he felt about being called a rapist. But all he did was wink at her. Beth felt it all the way to her toes. "Bethany, are you in there? Come here and open this door. Your father has a gun."

"I most certainly do not have a gun. Don't say things like that when not only is it not true, but for Christ's sake, you could get me killed. What if they shot me because you told them I was armed? Christ, Ruth, I swear you're not right in the head most of the time."

As they continued to argue, Beth stayed where she was. She supposed she could have gotten up and unlocked the door for them, but she really didn't want to. Maybe if it had been only her father, but her mother would find fault with everything in the home. Including the fact that she'd not done her dishes or even made her bed today. Some days it was just too much work, and she was here alone, so it mattered little to her if things were in tiptop shape. When Nate put his hands over hers again, she realized her heart was hurting.

"Just breathe." She nodded at his softly spoken words and felt herself calming a great deal. "In and out, Bethany. Just breathe in and out, and we'll be here for you should you need us to be."

"It's Beth. My mother is the only one that calls me that. And they fight all the time. I think it's why I needed to leave to do this on my own. My mom would have made me crazy, and I would have died sooner." He nodded and told her to breathe again. "Do you think if we just drove off, they'd realize it?"

"Not for a little while anyway. They're into each other pretty good right now. I don't know that they'd hear a bomb go off right next to them." She laughed when he did. "There's my girl. Feeling like you can take them now? If not, we can just sit here until the police arrive. They should be here soon for the other man, who isn't a rapist either."

It didn't even bother her that he'd mentioned her mother's rude behavior. Nor did she think he was what she'd called him. But to leave here, without her parents, was tempting. Very much so. But when their arguing took on a louder tone, she asked Chris to open the door. When he stood up to do so, Nate did as well. Both of them were protecting her. She had no idea why that thought popped into her head, but she knew as surely as she was still sitting there that's exactly what they were doing.

Her mom came huffing in first, then her dad. Standing up, she felt a little dizzy, but before she could sit again, Nate put his arms around her and held her. It was in that moment that Beth felt safe. Stronger, and even being a complete stranger, as he was, she knew that she could trust him with her life. Strength blanketed her, and she was not only able to walk to her parents on steady feet, but she didn't feel the urge to hold on to things to stand upright as she did so.

"Mom? Dad? What are you doing here? How on earth did you even find me?" She looked at her mom first, then her dad. "Dad, you didn't? You didn't give into her and come out here to be with me. I wish now that I'd not mentioned

31

which direction I was going, so she'd not brow beat it out of you. You should have told me what she'd done." Her dad wouldn't look at her, concentrating instead on the tiles of her floor.

Her mother glared at her dad, then huffed at her before she spoke. "You mean on that private phone that the two of you shared and didn't tell me about? What a thing to do to someone. It's not fair of you to have your own little private time without me. Bethany, I can see your father doing this, but you?" Beth looked at her mom and asked her how they were to have private time if she was included. But of course, her mom ignored that. "He left it out and I found it. Imagine my surprise when I figured out that he'd been calling you behind my back all this time. I'm sure that the two of you had a very good laugh over poor Mom worrying about her sick daughter."

"We rarely mentioned you, if you want to know the truth." She heard Nate laugh and then cough when her father spoke. "And you didn't just happen to find the phone because I left it out, you snooped around until you found it. I have no idea how you even got the safe open that I had it in. You can bet that I'm going to be changing that combination when we get home. But I didn't leave it out for you to find."

Chris cleared his throat and said the police were here, as was an ambulance. When he left them to go out, Nate excused himself and followed. Beth watched him leave her alone with her parents, and decided that she was a grown ass woman and started by her mom to go see what she could do to help the police. But her mom reached out and grabbed her arm and pulled her back hard enough that she stumbled against the counter.

"Where are you going? We need to plan and talk about

where we're going next. I swear to you, I never realized how far it was until we started out. Your father had to drive almost straight through to get this far. He was a real bear about it too, but I just had to see you. And I can tell now that you need me here with you. Like usual. I swear Bethany, you just don't think well enough ahead. Your father might not have had to work so hard and be so mean to me had you just let us go with you as I suggested in the first place." Her dad sat at the table and put his head in his hands, while her mom started pulling dishes out of the sink. "I'll just ride with you from now on. That way I can keep your house clean. This is because you don't have me here with you, Bethany; you're as sloppy as your dad."

"Don't touch my dishes." Her mom backed from the sink so quickly that she dropped one of the plates. Beth didn't even bother bending to pick it up, knowing that she'd be too dizzy to stand up with it. "These are my dishes, in my sink, in my home. Mine, I tell you. And you're not going to be riding with me, and you are most certainly not going to be making plans to travel any further than required for you to get off the highway and then back on the sucker. Now, I have to deal with the police, but I do expect you to leave my things alone. Do you hear me, Mother?"

"Yes, yes, I hear you. You're shouting loud enough. Bethany. You shouldn't get your temper up...how will you ever get better? I'm just going to tidy up a bit. You know how I love a clean home. It won't take me but a moment to have —"

"Touch anything in here and I will never speak to you again." Her mom smiled at her, as if she was nervous. "So help me, if I come back in here and there is one thing cleaned up that wasn't before, I will have that officer out there arrest you for trespassing. Get out of my home right now before I'm really pissed off."

"It's just doing the dishes, Bethany. And perhaps running the sweeper over this floor. I'll just do this and then you'll feel better about having me come and stay with you while we travel together. And so you know, Bethany, this is no way to talk to your mother. Tell her, Lyle. Tell her to calm down before I get upset. You know how I get when things aren't cleaned up." Her dad stood up, and she was sure he was going to smack her mom. But all he did was kiss Beth on the forehead before going out of the camper. "Well. I guess he's upset too. The dishes won't take a moment, then I'll go and see to your bed too. I bet that you've not—"

"Get out." Her mom grabbed the dishtowel that Beth had put on the sink when she'd been too weak to fuck with it. When she turned on the water, Beth smacked her hands away and then gave her a small but effective push. "I'm not kidding you, Mother. Get out of here right now or I will have you arrested."

"I don't know why you think you can speak to me this way, but I'm leaving. First your father is mean to me, and now you. My only daughter. I don't know what the big deal is—we're going to be living in this thing together, and it'll be better for us both if I just clean up—but I'll do it later. When you're less upset."

Beth started to say she wasn't going to do it later either, but decided she'd won this round and wouldn't crow. When her mom was out the door, Beth leaned against the table and made her body relax. It wasn't until arms wrapped around her waist that she realized she wasn't alone. She'd been so upset that she'd not even heard Nate coming in again.

"I have less than two months to live." She felt him nod. "I have a heart condition that will eventually kill me, and it won't be a pretty sight. My body will slowly shut down, starting with things like my kidneys and other internal organs. Then I'll just die."

"Is that why you left them behind? So you could die in peace?" She told him that had been the plan. "I don't think they're helping you much, especially your mom. Stress isn't anything you need right now. And by the way, you look a great deal like her. You're not at all like her, but you look like her."

"Thanks, I think. And no, she's not helping me at all. Mom has it in her head that I'm just sick and will get better soon, no matter how many times I tell her that I'm dying. And she won't believe me when I tell her I want to be left alone. Her constant harping on Dad hurts me, and she acts like the wounded bird when things don't go her way. Dad didn't want to do this; he told me so." Nate turned her in his arms and she looked up at him. "Why are you doing this for me? And for that matter, why am I no longer afraid that you're going to hurt me? I only just met you, and I feel like I've known you my whole life. What is this thing?"

"Trust." She nodded at him, not even sure why. "I'd very much like to kiss you right now. I'm not going to, but I want to. The police would like to talk to you, and I'm afraid that if I take you into my arms enough to taste that very pretty mouth of yours, we won't be leaving here for some time."

"You want to kiss and make love to me? As much as it terrifies me, I think I want the same thing. I don't understand this." He nodded and rocked into her, his body pressing her into the table briefly. "You're a stranger to me, and all I can think about is letting you make love to me. Touch me in places that only you would know arouse me."

"You're not making this any easier; you know that, don't

you?"

She found that she didn't want to make it any easier on him either. But when he pulled away from her, she moved to the door with him. Her heart, even had it been healthy, was going to be hurt, she knew it.

Chapter 3

Nate watched the three of them. Beth seemed to be in the middle of her parents all the time when they were together. Her father not so much, but her mom was a piece of work that seemed to thrive on being the victim even when she was usually the abuser. She was forever putting Lyle down, ridiculing him for one thing or another, and treating Beth as if not only would she get over this illness of hers, but she might, just a little, be faking it. When Ruth came to stand by him, he didn't try to diminish his size by slouching over as he normally would, but stood tall, and even went so far as to puff out his chest a little more. He had no desire to be in this woman's sights.

"You have no idea what I have to do to put up with her father every day when we're together. It's like he enjoys making me cry. I can't tell you how mean he is to me. And the things he says are just abusive and hurtful. Like he thinks I don't have any feelings at all. I don't know how much more I can take. I've asked Bethany to talk to him about it several times, but she takes his side every single time. Treating me like nothing more than dust in the corner." Nate said nothing, not even sure why she was sharing such information with him. "I would think that if you're dating my little girl, you'd be able to make Lyle see reason. Tell him to listen to me. I think you, being a big man like you are, would make him pay attention to me when I beg him to be nicer to me."

"You mean you want me to make him mind you?" She smiled at him and nodded. "No. I won't do that. He's a grown man. Not a five-year-old that has to have you telling him what to do all the time. Besides, from where I am, you're not a walk in the park to be around either." Nate thought she'd get upset, but all she did was move around what he'd said as if was unimportant because it wasn't getting her what she wanted.

"He never does what I tell him to. How am I supposed to get things done if I forever have to keep an eye on him so that he stays out of trouble? He's as bad as that couple down the street…they're forever dragging me into their messes. I just don't know what I'm supposed to do with the way people are just out to wreck their lives. I feel like a counselor most of the time." Nate watched Lyle talk to the police. He looked like he was articulate, intelligent, and seemed to have a good sense of humor. Ruth looked in the direction he was and tsked. "Just look at him. He is more than likely telling them every little thing I've done wrong to him when I've done nothing. They're going to lock him away one of these days, and I'll be tempted to just let them. No one understands what I have to put up with all day long."

"I'm sure that anyone you come in contact with knows every detail of what you think you have to put up with all the time." He saw the confusion on her face, as if she wasn't sure he was insulting or agreeing with her. "Perhaps if you're so unhappy with the way things are, you should just leave the marriage. Women have left their husbands for a great deal less than you think you're putting up with."

"Oh no. I could never leave him on his own. I don't think he's smart enough to be alone for any length of time, do you?

Why, there are any number of things he could get himself into trouble over if I'm not there to guide him. I'd be worried to death that he'd be into something that I've not approved of and end up in jail; or worse, he'd be dead. Poor man is a fool without me around to keep things right for him. What do you think would happen if I were to leave him? Chaos, complete and total chaos." Several things came to mind about what Lyle might do on his own, but Nate voiced none of them. "Besides, what would the neighbors think should I just up and leave him because he is stupid?"

He was saved from making a comment on that when Chris came back. Nate had no idea why he thought so, but he had a feeling Chris knew just what he'd been about to say to the woman. When he winked at him, he realized that he did. The man had more than likely saved him a great deal of trouble. Killing this broad would be bad news right now.

"The police said that once we get Beth's home up and running, we need to get her off the highway if we can. I explained to him about the overheating, and he said he could smell it so there's no problems there." Chris looked at Ruth. "He said that you and your husband need to get going now, as there is nothing wrong with your motor home, and it's dangerous for you to be parked here."

"That won't work for me. No, I'm not leaving my daughter out here to be on her own. Besides, she and I have made some plans for me to ride with her for a little while, just so I can get her house in order. She's just such a mess without me around. Almost as bad as her father, you know. You just go and tell him that we're having troubles too, and if he talks to my husband stop him." Chris looked at him then back at Ruth. "She's not feeling well and is my only child. Just tell him that. Then you can come back here and tell me what he said. But remember, don't let him talk to Lyle. He's not right in the head about such matters."

"If you are under the assumption that I'm your errand boy, then you really need to rethink that right now. First of all, your husband told them that the home you're in is in tiptop shape. Even went so far as to show them the improvements he's made on it so that it's in better condition than when it came off the assembly line. So if you want to lie to them, you go right on ahead and get your ass in trouble. But leave me out of it." Ruth's lower lip started to shake and her eyes filled with fake tears. She was good, Nate would give her that. And Chris saw right through her as well. "Honey, I've been in front of bigger monsters than you can even imagine. You don't scare me one bit. So, get your skinny little ass in your motor home and get your whiney self on down the road like you were told nicely."

"I won't have you talking to me this way. I'm a grown woman and I demand that you treat me as such." Chris told her to start acting like it then. When she turned to Nate, he knew this was going to get nasty quickly. "I would very much appreciate it if you'd ask your friend to be nicer to me. He has no idea the trials that I've had to put up with coming all the way out here. And then to have him insult me."

"Your trials are about to be compounded in ways you cannot fathom, Mrs. Snow, and you're going to pretty much be pissed off for a long while if you try that shit on the others that I live with. So I would suggest you do as he said before he changes into his big dragon and ends this world of your nastiness." She looked at Chris, and Nate knew then that she was not only aware of just shifters, but more than likely had known a few of them personally. Nate wondered how that had gone over and why she'd not been killed yet. Shifters were not a tolerant group of people. Smiling, he wondered if he could convince Skylar, or maybe even Jamey, to take care of her for him. "Ruth, he's barely holding onto his animal, and I am so close to releasing mine as well. Go to your camper."

She stalked away and Nate looked at Chris. When he shook his head, Nate looked down the road to Beth. She was upset again, not because of anything that was going on with them, but he'd bet that it had a great deal to do with her mom. He looked at Chris.

"Can you take my truck back to the compound? I'm going to see if she'll let me drive the camper in instead of letting her mom be with her. I don't know for sure if her parents can cross over the barrier—she is one bitch of a woman, that mom of hers—but I'd feel better if Beth was with us." Chris said he could do that and they both walked to her camper just as her dad and mom drove around them. Nate looked into the large front window.

Ruth was gesturing with her hands wildly and her mouth was moving a mile a minute, while Lyle was driving with his body slumped over the wheel like a man waiting for the ax to come down on his neck. Nate so would not want to be that man right now. He'd bet anything she was telling the poor man what a failure he was not to mention stupid. A name that she seemed to like to call her husband.

"She's dying...you know that, don't you?" He nodded at Chris as they poured water into the radiator now that it had cooled off enough. "I can detect a heart problem, and while I'm not a doctor, I'm thinking it's pretty serious. Do you suppose when you take her that she'll be all right? I mean, do you think it will cure whatever it is?"

"I don't know. And so you know, I'm not going to have sex with her. Not intercourse, anyway." He asked him why not. "Because, in the event you didn't notice, I outweigh her by a good hundred and fifty pounds and I'm well over a foot taller than her. Can you imagine what I could do if I tried to fuck her? I'm not going to do that to her."

"I don't think it works that way, Nate." Nate said nothing. "So how do you think that's going to go? I mean, I know what you are, and I'm pretty sure that at some point you're going to have to claim her as your mate. You know as well as I do that only happens if you're having sex with her. Also, I'd really like to know why you think your weight has a damned thing to do with sex with Beth."

They both turned when they heard a sharp intake of breath. He had no idea how long Beth had been there, but he was sure that it was both too long and not long enough. If she heard the entire conversation, he might be able to salvage something. If she only heard the last part, he was fucked. When he took a step toward her, she took several back. He could tell that she was upset, but when she nodded once, he wasn't sure how to take that either.

"The officer said that I could go, but I needed to remain close to answer questions." Nate nodded, not taking his eyes off her. "I'm assuming that I can get to the campground now without any problems? Thank you for fixing that for me, by the way."

"This is only a temporary fix, I'm afraid. You have a hole in your radiator." Nate looked at Chris. There wasn't a hole in it; it just needed some extra water. "Nate here knows a bit about engines, and he wants you to take it back to the garage and let him have a look at it for you before taking off again."

"I don't think so. You've been very nice, but I have to be on my way." Chris handed him the jug in his hand and walked to the truck. Nate said nothing as Chris drove around them and beeped his horn as he did so. "What does he think is going to happen now? I'm just going to let you ride with me to your supposed garage and you can both kill me?"

"Back to not trusting again, are you? And why do you jump to me killing you every time? I can understand it, but have I ever given you any reason to think I'd hurt you? I'm pretty sure, had I wanted to, you'd be dead by now. Yet here you stand." Nate turned to the camper and finished putting the water in. "I don't know shit about cars other than they get me from one point to the next. But I do know that you're not well and that your parents, your mom in particular, is going to drive you over the edge if she is allowed to ride alone with you for any length of time. Either in this motor home or theirs."

"She's just worried." Nate turned and looked at her. "Okay, she's a mean, nasty person, but she is my mom. And trust me when I tell you, she is not going to be doing any riding with me any more than you are."

"She is your mom, and I'd not count on the latter if I were you." He capped the jug. "I'd very much like to explain what you walked into just now. I'm not going to hurt you. Or have sex with you."

"Why not? I mean, why would you even think that would ever…? I never said that I wanted to…. You know what, never mind. I don't care. It's not going to happen." He felt his heart twist up in his chest and put his hand over the pain. "How are you going to get back to your place? And if you tell me that you'll have to hitch a ride with me, that's not going to win you any brownie points either."

"I could fly back, I guess. Or shift and take the backwoods so no one shoots me. I can be just about anything I want. Eagle. Wolf. Bear. Which is my favorite animal to become." She took a step back, but didn't deny that he could shift if he wanted. It made him think things were going to go a little easier. He hoped anyway. "Good, so like your mom, you know a few shifters. I'm one, as well as Chris and the rest of us. I'm an elite shifter. Do you know what that is?"

"No. I don't know what you're talking about. You've made a mistake." He said nothing but stared at her. "Can you really fly?"

"Yes. I can become a hawk, as I said, or any larger birds of prey. And if that doesn't work, I can become any other animal that walks on four legs. Also, when I need to, and it has to be very necessary, I can become someone else. I can't talk like them, and sometimes I don't know how they move, but I can do it. However, it's very draining on me. Being able to shift, as I said, has saved my ass a few times to not be human." She looked around then back at him. "I won't hurt you. Not ever. How much do you know about shifters?"

"I knew a lion shifter a while back. But he and his mate moved away. They were very nice and loved each other dearly, or so it seemed. Is that what the two of you were talking about, you and Chris? You think I'm your mate or something?" He nodded. "I'm dying, soon. As my heart gets larger, trying to supply my body with blood, it kills me faster. I was given only about six months, so I have a couple of months at most. If I'm to understand this mate thing, I'm it for you. What will happen to you if...when I die?"

"You won't die if you let me help you." She shook her head and backed from him. "You know that with only my touch you feel better, stronger. And my blood is extremely powerful. A sip can make your heart better and you stronger as well. You're weak now. I can feel it. All you want to do is go inside and take a nap."

"I do, more than anything, but I won't until you're gone. I think it's important that you understand what is going to happen to me. As this gets worse, I will tire more and more. Soon, I don't know when, I won't even be able to get out of bed to shower or go to the bathroom. My heart is working too hard to keep me going as it is. But I won't let you *try* and prolong my life. It's too hard on those that I'm leaving behind to give them false hope. Because that would be all it is, correct?" He shook his head and took a small step toward her as he asked her if that was why she was running. "Yes. My parents, I couldn't do this to them. Let them see me grow weaker. My dad...he's my world."

"Let me help you." She shook her head but he could tell she wanted it. "Go into the camper, love, and get in bed. I'll take you to the compound where I live, and there's a doctor there, Weston Page. He can tell you how long you have should you not let me help you. He's brilliant, and trustworthy as well."

"You mean that he'll tell me what you want me to know." Nate took another step toward her. "Please don't hurt me. I know that I'm going to die and all, but I don't want to be hurt."

"I won't hurt you."

He picked her up in his arms and took her inside. Nate was surprised at how much room was in this thing, and the bed was huge. Laying her on it, he covered her up and then kissed her on the forehead. When she closed her eyes, he left her there and went to the front. He'd been driving one of the bigger cargo trucks, so he was pretty sure he could handle this thing. Sitting behind the steering wheel for a few seconds, he let out a long slow breath.

"She's my mate," he said softly. "And she's not well.

45

When the fates fuck with you, they really know how to run you through the ringer, I guess."

Starting the motor home, he turned on the signal to indicate he was merging into traffic. As he made his way to the compound, he reached out to Skylar and Remy to let them know what was going on. They told him that Weston would be ready for him when he got there.

~~~

When she woke up, not only was she not in her home, but she had no clue where she was at all. Sitting up carefully, she noticed the room was hospital like and that Nate was sitting in the chair across the room, stretched out with his long legs in front of him. She knew instinctively that he wasn't asleep. When he sat up and looked at her, she pulled the sheet up over her.

"I can go and get Weston if you want." Beth asked him where she was. "The compound where I live. When I got you here I was worried when you didn't wake right away. Then after an hour I got really worried and had you brought in here. You never once stirred. Weston said that it was because you've been doing too much and it took you under."

"I get tired really easy nowadays." He nodded. "I don't know what you mean by the compound. You've said that to me before. Where is that exactly?"

"It's a place where we all live and work. Mostly we work, but lately we've been having a lot more down time. I guess because Benton hasn't shown himself, even though we know that he's around." She put up her hand. He laughed. "I'm guessing that was too much. I'm nervous too."

"Benton?" He explained who that was. "So he's the big guy that you're all fighting. And this Benton person, he's responsible for making these other things too, you said. But I don't know what you mean about malefactors nor the others. Adherents?"

"Yes, that's it. He created them as sort of an army. But they seemed to be too stupid to control. But they did kill a great many humans. Changing them into what he was. Have you noticed, the closer you got to where I picked you up that there were fewer people? A few abandoned cars along the way? Perhaps you've seen things that sort of made you second guess yourself?" She told him she had. "He did it. Benton, he calls himself Master, he and these other two men, Dolin and Ward, created a group of beings that were to come here and take over the world for them. And in doing so, they not only killed off a lot of the human race in this area, but also changed quite a few into killing monsters, much like they were."

She thought of this person, Master. Something tugged at her memory until she had to close her eyes for a moment and think. Then it occurred to her why it had been familiar. She looked at Nate.

"This Benton person, is he a big winged creature? Has large claws that he uses to swing at people?" He nodded. "I dreamed about him. Several times, as a matter of fact. I might not have equated him with the name, but he kept calling himself Master all the time. And he wanted everyone else to also. I just thought it was the drugs I was taking. Do you suppose that would be the same man?"

"That would be him." Nate stood up then and started pacing. She noticed that he was extremely careful as to where he stepped. "What happens when you dream of him? I mean, who do you see and what is going on?"

"There are others with you, and... I'm there. I have a sword, and I'll tell you now, I've never held one before, so I have no idea where that might have come from. But there is a dragon...no, that's not right—there's two of them. But they sort of merge together sometimes. Most everyone has wings, including you. There is a giant cat...panther, I think. Also a man and woman that are completely covered in tattoos. Like yours, but different."

"You can see mine." Nodding, she watched his face. He looked afraid...or excited, she wasn't sure. "Do you know any of their names? Do we call out to each other when you dream about him?" Nodding, Beth had a feeling that this wasn't just a run of the mill dream she'd been having. She might have been able to convince herself of that if he didn't seem to believe every word out of her mouth. "Tell me who they are, and I'll bring them here so that you can see if they're the same person in your dreams."

"Rembrandt, but he goes by several names...mostly Remy. Skylar. They're the two that are sort of in charge. Vicki and Davis, again, a couple. There are others. The man from today, his name is Chris, he's one of the dragons. The woman, the other one, I don't think I know her name."

"Her name is Jamey. So when you asked about Chris in the motor home when we were talking to you, you thought you knew him." Beth told him that it only just occurred to her, but thought it was because of the accident. "Yes, I can understand that. The rest? Are there others?"

"Yes, but I don't know their names. And if I did, I don't know them now." She got up to pace, and she noticed that he seemed to try and shrink down in size. "You're very self-conscious of your size, aren't you?"

"I am. I don't want to accidently hurt you in any way. And I worry about that. I'm a big person, and when I shift into my other animals, they're bigger too. I was drugged against my will." She nodded, remembering something about a cage, and asked him about it. "Yes. In another realm. I was taken there as a test subject. The drug made me stronger as well. If there is more to it, I'm not sure what it would be just yet."

The door opened and there stood Remy and Skylar. Neither of them looked confused. In fact, Remy looked as if he'd been told a great joke and was still thinking of it when he sat in the chair that Nate had been in. Skylar looked amused as well, but she was more…laid back, Beth thought. As if she knew she was bad-assed and didn't care who knew it.

But these people had been in her dreams. And now, here they were standing before her. Beth looked at Nate. She wanted him to tell her it was a joke, that he'd somehow, she didn't know how, conjured them up just for her.

"I don't know what's going on." He nodded. "I thought I was having bad dreams. Even before I got ill, I knew that something was wrong with me, having dreams about a group of people that I didn't know. And you could do things…things that aren't humanly possible that scared me."

"We're not human. None of us are." Skylar sat on the edge of the bed when Beth sat down, and stared at her as if she were trying to analyze a bug under a microscope. "You're very ill. I mean, close to dying ill, aren't you?"

"I have an enlarged heart that is killing me." Skylar nodded. "You can fly. And you have a sword on your back that looks like a tattoo but isn't, don't you?"

"Yes. I have wings and all sorts of magic." She put out her hand. "I can help you. Not heal you, but I can help enough that I can prolong your life for some time. Nate can heal you completely, but you'd have to trust him. But you don't, do you?"

Beth looked at the offered hand, then at Skylar again. "At what cost? I'm sure that it's not as simple as you touching me and that'll help. What will I have to repay to take this from you?"

"Repay? Nothing. Unless you consider friendship a form of payment. But as to what else you'll gain? I don't know, but I'm sure there will be more than just simply some help. What it would be, I have no idea. But I do know that if you let me, I can help." Beth looked at Nate and he nodded. She had no idea why, but she knew this man, of all the people in this place, was someone that would never harm her. "None of us will ever harm you, Beth. Never. We've just had it pointed out to us that we're a family. An odd one, but family all the same. And as far as we're concerned, you're as much a part of this family as everyone else is."

"Ryiah. I remember her name now. She told you that." Skylar nodded, then looked at Nate. "No, he didn't tell me. I have been having dreams about you and the rest of the people here. A while back...I'm not sure when, but a woman was killed. Her heart was pulled from her chest by Remy. A little boy was ill. A child was born that isn't human. All kinds of things are coming to me that I thought...I guess hoped, was just a dream caused by the drugs they have me on."

Her chest hurt; Beth could feel her vision starting to narrow and fizz out. Reaching out blindly for anything, her hand connected with someone's and she knew that it was Skylar's. Then hands were on her shoulder, her head, moving over her in a comforting yet firm way. As she was laid back on the bed, Beth knew something else...for now, she was going to be all right. But there were consequences of the touch too. Too many for her mind to hold onto.

Closing her eyes to the onslaught of images that seemed to be right in front of her, she saw it all, the death of them. The monster that caused it. Remy had his head removed, and

Beth knew that was the only way to end such a warrior's life. Skylar was killed the same way. The swipe of a great claw from the monster removed her head from her body.

Davis and his mate, Vicki, were taken out, their bodies crushed beneath the monster's foot, wings torn apart as their heads rolled away. They had swords that had done them little good against the monster's great strength.

Leo was snapped out of the sky by the powerful mouth of the monster. He was chewed up then swallowed down in the hot belly of acid. Jamey, without her mate, the other half of her dragon, fell to the earth, dead. They were as connected as tightly as a single tree, and the death of one meant the same for the other.

Chris, as his cat, was sliced in half. It wasn't until he fell to the earth, his body bleeding and spent, that she realized that his own mate had met the same fate. Kate, his beautiful Kate, died with him. Then the monster stepped on them, digging his sharp claws into their heads and ending all hope of either of them helping their other half.

Rick and Ryiah, even with their considerable army of faeries, could not defeat the thing that had come for them. Thousands of them at a time fell to the earth, their wings tattered, their bodies mutilated. Even their queen suffered, the death of so many taking a huge toll on her magic. Rick made a move to his mate, Ryiah to him. They were killed even as they touched, their fingers together showing their powerful love for each other.

"Tell me." She heard the voice, deep and full of emotion, as the images slowed, the sounds, loud before, muted when Nate spoke to her as she dreamt. "Tell me what you see when we die. You see it, tell me."

"You're a great bear; your body is beaten, your arm

broken. I am there with you, my sword hitting the monster in the belly, his blackened heart and soul. But we cannot defeat him, he's killing us all. There is something holding us back, something that we're missing." Skylar asked her what they'd done wrong, how had they lost. "We were separate. We fought and lost to him because we weren't one. We're not family."

The darkness took her. The exhaustion of simply seeing the images, what they told her, took her under. Her last thought as she slipped away was that she was a part of something huge, and she was going to lose it before she understood it fully.

Chapter 4

Master flew back and forth over the mountains, loving the way his body seemed to just glide effortlessly. He supposed that he did that well...he was perfect in his estimation. Master felt wonderful. Stronger than he thought he ever had, and he seemed to be getting stronger daily. As he dove into the depths of the water again, loving the way it made him feel, he was careful of not going too deep or fast. He'd learned that lesson the hard way, and would not want a repeat of that any time soon.

Just yesterday he had thought to take a nice swim. No matter how he felt when he entered the watery depths, he always felt better when he emerged. But he'd been a little... overzealous, he thought now, and had dove head first into the water. The bottom had come up much faster than he'd thought it would, and he'd had to work nearly twenty minutes to free his head from the mud and mire. Then nearly that much longer to clean it from his ears. That was when he'd come to a startling revelation.

The water wasn't as deep. He had no idea how that was happening, nor when it had taken place. But yesterday he had to lay flat in the water, along the muddy bottom, to cover his entire body. And today was much worse. He'd had to take handfuls of it to cover some of his bigger parts, his wings and feet. As he lay there, he tried to think if he'd had to do this before and knew that he was right. Someone was taking his water without permission.

Not that he would have given it to anyone to take the water, but should they had wanted it, even a sip, he might have relented. Perhaps not, but he might have. But now someone was taking his precious water, and that wasn't right. He was master of all his domain right now, and he wasn't happy to know that someone was taking what was rightfully his.

Rising his head above it, he looked around. There were deer on the shoreline, but Master didn't think there were nearly enough of them to begin to drain his waterway. And he'd never seen even one of them with a large bucket, so he took them off the list. Master looked around the entire shoreline and saw a bear and her cubs, a moose, as well as a few wolves that he'd been sure would never return after he'd scared them off a few days ago. None of them, however, were large enough to take as much water as he seemed to be missing.

"It's Rembrandt, he's doing this to you because he does not want you to be well, nor does he want you to win your war. You know this, correct?" He told Dolin that he wasn't sure. "He's dammed up your water so he can keep it all for himself and that woman of his. That can be the only explanation. You know that the deer aren't doing it. It has to be him."

"Do you really think he could have done this?" Dolin told him that Rembrandt seemed to forever be more resourceful than anyone they'd ever encountered. "He does have magic that gets stronger all the time. What do you suppose he has done to stop my flow? Surely he cannot call down the mountains to do as he wishes. I should have such power, not him. He is nothing. I am Master."

"I believe that is just what he has done; he's called down the mountain to do as he wishes. That woman with the white fingers, do you suppose she had that sort of power to help him? It is most unfair of him to have so many people helping when you have only myself and Ward." Master didn't say it aloud, but he thought them not so useful. "I think you should go there and confront him about this. Tell him to let the water come to you again and that he shouldn't be doing such a thing. Also, I've been thinking about the people he has with him. Perhaps you can have him give you part of the people that work for him. Make it even. However, you should have the strongest of his group. You are master of all."

"No, no. I have my plan worked out to defeat Rembrandt and his woman. And when I am at my strongest, I will go there and demand that he gives everything over to me, including his people. They would not be able to work for a dead man anyway, and they could serve me much better." Dolin said that if the water was depleting, that he might not ever get to his peak strength. "Yes, there is that. I have to think on this."

His plan was perfect now. He was going to catch them unguarded, since he was sure that they believed him dead when he'd disappeared like he had. They'd hurt him too, badly, but now he was better. Much more than he'd ever been. His plan, he knew, was going to make him ruler of all.

Master was going to fly over them, blowing his hot flames all over the place, and pick them off one at a time when they ran for the edges of the magic. There was the magical dome that was there, but he had a feeling that it was only up and working when he wasn't around. They would be lax in their being prepared for him. And because of that, he was going to kill them, one at a time, and not allow them to touch him with magic or swords again.

"How do you know they think you're dead?" Master almost cringed away from the sound of Mary's voice. He had noticed that everyday her voice got more harpy like, and shriller. He disliked her very much now. "You know as well as I that he has spies everywhere. I'm betting right now that one of those animals there are one of his men that makes you only think they're an animal. Perhaps he's the buck or the wolf. You did run them off, and yet here they are again."

"No, Rembrandt is not changing into animals. It would not be fair if he could, would it? No, you're wrong. Again. I have not allowed him to be able to change into animals, so he cannot. It is hard enough fighting him when he is a mere man. To be able to change, well, that would be most unfair of him. I would have to have such an ability too. He'll have to share how that is done." Mary snorted at him. "Why are you so negative to me? Can you not just be nice to me and agree once in a while?"

"If you were ever right, yes, I could agree with you. But since that is so seldom, I find myself simply disagreeing with you every time you open your mouth. It saves time." He would gladly kill her now if she wasn't already dead. "Go there, Benton, and take care of him now. You think this is going to be going on forever? I have things to do that do not require me hanging around with you all the time."

"You are dead. What can you have to do that would require you not being here with me? I think you are here just to irritate me. I do not understand why you do not just go away. I have no use for your advice, nor do I care for your meanness to me. Why must you treat me this way? I am Master." She snorted, and he lifted his body from the water and watched the animals that had come here to drink scatter. "See? They know what I am to them. Master of all. Why can you not believe it when I tell you the same?"

She said nothing, and he felt as if he'd won a round with her. He'd have to keep on his guard more now. It was getting harder to get the better of her, and she never shut up. Even when he was sleeping, she seemed to be right there. Master watched the creatures as they thought themselves hidden from him, and did wonder, just a little, if any of them could be a man that turned into a beast. It bore thinking about.

He moved slowly toward the encampment. He'd been here several times over the last few days, just to watch, make sure that no one else joined them, and that they'd not gotten any stronger. Master was disappointed to see them out in the yard working, at practice with their swords and other weaponry as if they'd be ready for him. They did not seem to be growing lax in their effort to harm him in any way at all. He was sure that they would have been lounging about and going over the border of their land all the time now that they thought him dead.

He watched Rembrandt as he worked his swords with another man. The two of them seemed to have perfected their play, even to the point where they would start over and over if there was one thing that they seemed to think not right. To Master, it looked as if they were the best he'd ever seen. But of course he would never say that to them. He would say that they were imperfect, as well as clumsy in their work. Giving them more of a large head would not do.

"Do you think that if you were to show yourself now that they'd run for cover?" He told Ward that he thought not. They were too focused on what they were doing, and would perhaps hurt him if given the chance. "I think you might be right, now that you mention it. They are in the mood to harm someone, and while I think they cannot hurt you as you are after your water treatments and rest, there is no point in showing them how strong you are now."

"I wish every day that I had killed Rembrandt when I'd had the chance." Ward asked him when that might have been. "When he lay over his wife's grave sobbing like a small child. I should have driven a stake through his heart and been done with him. To think, I was given the chance and I didn't take it. Oh, to be able to go back now and do so."

"I'm sorry, Benton, but should you have tried then, you would have surely died. You were not as perfect as you are now. Nor were you as brave and smart." He agreed with Ward. "I think that should you show yourself to them now, they might stand in fear and you could take them out once and for all. There is the matter of them having the stones that you need to make an army."

"I'm not making an army, Ward. I have told you this over and over. I shall take him on myself and win. He is no longer stronger than me, nor I believe is he as smart. Not that he'd ever been, but now I am smarter by far. I have gotten something more from that water than even I can imagine happening." That didn't sound right, but he let it go. Just lately, over the last day or so, Master had begun to hear words coming out of his mouth that made no sense, strung together like laundry on a clothes line. He snapped his thoughts down. He didn't like the places that his mind was going of late.

Just last night he'd had a horrible thought. Rembrandt had won, and in doing so, he'd killed him. Master had woken from the dream in a hot sweat, his body hurting from his harsh breathing and painful head. Rembrandt could not win. He would not, as far as Master could think.

"When you kill him, I so wish I could be there with you." Master asked him what he would do. "I should like to ask him why he murdered our poor Mary. She was such a good soul."

Master had other opinions of Mary, and not a one of them made him think of her as good at anything but nagging. She did that well. As he watched the men on the field, Master thought of the other dreams that he'd been having. Ones that had him the victor as well as ruler. It was a dream that he so enjoyed when he woke that he wished, at times, he could sleep all the day.

"I kill them all. Not easily, mind, but I do win." He frowned when he thought of the second dream he'd had again, the one that had woken him with a scream spilling from his lips. "They are puny in comparison to my strength, don't you think, Ward? When I kill them one at a time, I will then burn their compound down with the others within their walls."

At least that was what had happened in his dreams until the last time. He couldn't remember all the details that had frightened him so badly. He'd been fighting them, swiping his mighty claws at them one at a time. Crushing them beneath his great weight, then they'd done something. He could not remember what it had been…his mind was so afraid of them that he could no longer think of the thing. But they had harmed him. Taking out first his magic, then his strength. He'd not yet spoken to any of his friends about it, fear of it coming to pass making him keep his thoughts to himself.

"Do you suppose when this is finished that we will be happy here in this realm?" He asked Dolin what he meant. "I should like to live here, if I wasn't dead. I wonder, at times like this, if we could come up with a drug to bring us back from the dead. There should be something that you can do to make that happen. Perhaps you can think of something for me. We could have such fun, Ward, you, and I. Don't you think so?"

Master wanted to point out that their bodies were not

here. That they'd died in another realm far from this place. Also, he wasn't sure that if they were alive with him that he'd be allowed to be in charge, rule as he wished. He didn't say anything about either of those thoughts, knowing that if he said as much to poor Dolin he would sulk for days. Ward might get angry, but over it quickly. But Dolin would be a baby about it.

"I shall think on that," was all he said.

Turning his back on the group, he made his way to the cave he'd been living in. Master laid upon his large stone after putting a fire to his pit, and thought of when he was going to go and kill Rembrandt. It was all he thought about now, and he had to get it done so that he might move on to being master of all. He looked over at his plan, all of it drawn out in detail so that he'd know just what to do. But the last panel to his plan, the one he'd drawn yesterday, had him lying on the ground and his body broken and dead. He didn't even know why he'd drawn such a thing.

"Motivation." Yes, he told Ward, he knew that was what it was. He had to keep himself thinking of what could happen should he not do as he'd planned. And since he was going to, the panel he'd drawn only served to make him stronger.

Closing his eyes, just a little afraid that he'd think of the other dream he'd had, he let sleep take him. He made himself take a nap daily, sometimes twice a day, to make sure that he was in tiptop shape. He decided, just before sleep claimed him, that he'd attack in two days. Just two days and he'd be master of all.

~~~

Nate saw Ruth before she saw him. Ruth and Lyle Snow had shown up the day before yesterday, and he'd been avoiding them as much as possible. Not so much Lyle, he thought, but the mother he was at all costs. The woman was caustic, and she was simply too whiney for his tastes. When someone stood beside him, he glanced over at Lyle and wondered if he thought him odd.

"I have been speaking to your man, Remy. He's very intelligent, isn't he?" Nate noticed that his voice was just a whisper, and answered him the same way. "I think perhaps that my daughter will be safer here than out on her own. I'm to understand that you have an excellent doctor on staff."

"Weston Page. Yes, he's very brilliant, and he has all the equipment needed to help her. And she will be fine with me as well." Lyle nodded. "Your wife, she thinks that Beth will recover from this heart issue soon. Is that true?"

"No. She's going to die. Soon, too, if the doctors at home were correct. Which I have no doubt they are. Her heart is working too hard to keep her alive, and it will give up soon. It's exhausted, I guess you could say." Nate had talked to Weston for a long time after Beth had gotten here. He said that with Skylar's help, even after her magic helped, Beth only had a few weeks to live. Unless he mated her. "You're not human, are you? I don't think any of you are, but you're not."

"No. I'm an elite shifter. I can take the shape of anything or anyone I wish. I'm also enhanced by a drug that was injected into me some time ago. It's why I'm so fucking huge." Lyle laughed and looked at him. "I'm sure you've talked to the others; Skylar must have explained to you what we're about."

"She did. As have the others. Hector, I don't think I caught his last name, he told me that he's from another realm. Very hard to pin down what he meant by that, but I'm assuming that he's not going to be able to say something to make me understand. He's very literal." Nate said that he was. "Beth is your mate, isn't she?"

"She is. I want you to know that I won't hurt her." Lyle said that he knew that too. "But I won't take her to my bed. I can't. I'd kill her quicker than her heart might."

"You think so?" Nate said nothing, suddenly uncomfortable with the conversation. "I spoke to her earlier. She was making plans to move on without us. I think I might like to be with her, but her mother would want to go as well. And I have a feeling that neither of them will survive being in the same vehicle for very long. Perhaps less than ten minutes, I would guess."

"She can't leave here." Lyle asked him what was keeping her here. "She's my mate. I cannot allow her to go."

"Can't allow her to go, huh? I'm not sure if you honestly believe you could keep her here or not, but I'd not say that to Beth. But if she didn't want to stay, know this…I'd stop you from trying to make her bend to your rules." Nate started to tell him that he'd never try to change her when Ruth turned and looked at them both. "Now, if you could see your way to getting her to leave, without her mom, I'd be a happy man and do just about anything for you."

"Lyle, what are you doing out here? I thought for sure that you were lying down for a nap." Lyle said nothing, but Nate could tell that he wanted to. "Oh Nate, you have no idea what I have to do to keep this man healthy. And the things he says to me when I try. It's like I'm trying to raise him up from a child on some days. No one knows what I have to endure nowadays."

"I don't need a nap, and the only reason I go to my room is to get away from you. I'm as healthy as a horse, Ruth. I might even be better if you were to leave me alone. And I'm a grown man; if I want to take a nap, I certainly don't need you to tell me to do so." She only waved him off. Lyle turned and walked away. Ruth looked at her husband before turning to Nate.

"I don't know what I'm to do with him. He's not doing anything that I tell him to. I had a talk with Bethany about him, but she refuses to tell him to do as I say. I swear to you, no one knows the things he does every day. And I have to go behind him and remind him of everything or he'd go out of the house without being dressed up sometimes."

"You mean that he wants to leave the house naked?" She looked at him crossly but shook her head. "Then I don't understand you."

"I lay out things for him to wear every day and he just ignores them. Even when I hide his ratty clothing, he finds more and wears them out where people can see him. I think he's losing his mind and simply doesn't care what others think about him." She tsked several times. "And when I make just the littlest of fusses over it, he blows up like I've asked him to do something horrible. It's just terrible the way he treats me at times, and I don't do a thing about it either."

"I just bet you don't. Perhaps you should just let him wear what he wants when he wants. And I think I'd be pissed at you as well if you treated me like I was ten and not an adult. What if he laid out your things to wear?" She asked him why he'd do that, she could make good sound decisions. "So can he, I'm betting."

"You have no idea what you're talking about. He's not right in the head. I've been carrying him for years now." Nate doubted that. "And even when I don't say anything much, he flies off the handle and is terribly mean to me. Then when I cry and cry, he acts like it's not important that he's made me so upset...acts as if my feelings or concerns don't matter one bit. I want you to know something else, too, I'm afraid of him.

I fear that he's going to be so mean to me once he'll hit me."

It was on the tip of his tongue to tell her he would have already done it. But he didn't. It was not that he thought she was right, because he thought she was stupid if she thought that Lyle needed her harping on him all the time. And when she asked him to have a talk with Lyle, tell him to listen to her, Nate walked away. He might have to get in the middle of this sometime, but not now. Instead he went to see how Beth was doing.

He found her in the kitchen with Ann. They were making some sort of sweet thing; he thought it was cookies, but he was told it was scones. To him sweet was sweet no matter what the shape ended up being. But when Ann left them alone, saying she wanted to check on her grandson, he sat down carefully in the chair and watched Beth.

"I talked to your dad. He seems to think that you plan to move on soon." She nearly dropped the bowl she had in her hand. "I'd rather you didn't."

"My mother put you…. Never mind. You'd not do a thing she wanted you to, and I'm glad for that. But if I stay, which I have no intention of doing, I'm just going to die here. And no offense, I have no desire to be on my deathbed with strangers around." He wasn't sure how much of a stranger she was to the household, but said nothing. Everyone he'd talked to had said that they'd talked to Beth and just loved her. "I don't want my mom around either. I don't think she's helping me."

"No, she's not. She asked me to have a talk to your father, tell him that he has to mind her like he's a child or something." She nodded, but he could tell she was upset. The eggs she was breaking into the bowl looked like they'd been crushed, not broken. "She told me that she lays out his clothing and he refuses to wear them. When I pointed out that maybe he

64

should do the same for her, she got upset and told me she could lay out her own things. Your mom is certifiable, I think."

"You're right on that. He was going to the grocery store once, just to pick up a gallon of milk. She laid out what she thought he should wear down there; a shirt, tie, and a jacket. And he didn't even bother with them. As he was going out the door, dressed comfortably, she called him back to ask what he thought he was doing. I guess she figured that he'd not seen them or something." Nate would bet not only had he seen them, but had tossed them to the floor. "When they went in his room, there was all the clothing wadded up and in the trash. She asked him what had happened to them."

"I bet he had a great deal to say about them." Beth laughed and nodded. "You're beautiful when you smile like that. You should do it more often."

"Anyway, when she asked him why they were wadded up, he told her that if he had wanted to wear a tie to the store for a gallon of milk, that someone should bring the milk out to him and have it encased in a golden carafe. Needless to say that didn't go over well." Nate watched her measure the other ingredients. "She called me, sobbing about it. How he wasn't listening to her and that he treated her so mean. Mean. She is forever telling everyone how mean he is, when in actuality, I think she's the nastiest person I know."

The urge to kiss her made him stand up. When she backed from him, he took a step back from her as well. He knew that she might be afraid of him...not that he blamed her, but he didn't want her to be. As he started to turn and leave the room before he did something stupid like pull her into his arms, she came closer to him.

"That day in the camper, I felt that you wanted me. I think that I'd like for you to touch me. At least kiss me." He took another step back from her. "You don't have to if you don't want to."

"I'd very much like to kiss you. All over your body. Take your pussy in my mouth, feed from your hot juices." He could smell her then, her arousal. "Your body is ready for mine. Wet and hot, isn't it?"

"It is. I think of you taking me all the time. Not just eating me, though that sounds wonderful, but you inside of me. Taking me to heights that I've never felt. I know that I haven't known you long, but you're all I can think about." He put out his hands when she was closer, meaning only to push her back. But he touched her breasts and felt them swell under his fingers when she moaned. "I need you. I don't know why, but I think you want me as well."

"I do." He cupped her breast in his hand and lifted it up, feeling the hard peak beneath her bra. "Would you let me feast on you? Take you into my mouth and drink deeply from you?"

"Please."

He only wrapped his arm around her waist, careful not to squeeze her too much, and willed them to his room. He kissed her then, again careful of what he was doing. And when he asked her to lay back on his bed, he wanted to strip down and take her then. But he couldn't. Not ever.

Stripping her of the soft jersey pants and sweatshirt she wore, he looked at her laying there. Her bra barely covering her breasts; her panties, a small triangle of silk and soaked with her juices, over her pussy. Pulling them down and off her legs, Nate went to the floor and took the silk to his nose and inhaled deeply. *Mine*, his mind screamed at him, she was his in all ways. But he'd never take all of her. Not so long as he was looking like this.

Chapter 5

His hands were large and strong, yet he was as gentle with her as if she was a newborn kitten. Every time his skin touched hers, all she wanted to do was beg him for more. When he leaned to her pussy, his breath hot on her thighs, she felt her body tense up for the feel of him touching her.

"Will you come for me?" Beth nodded and felt her body shudder in response to his words. "To taste you like this, spread out like a feast, all I can think about is how many times I want you to come down my throat."

"You have to take me, Nate. I need you to." He nodded and stuck out his tongue and ran it over her swollen clit. She came twice while he played with her, and she wondered how hard she would come when he finally took her. But when he buried his mouth over her, his tongue deep in her pussy, Beth screamed out her release and held onto the sheets. Christ, she thought, he was going to kill her when he finally took her.

His tongue fucked her, his hands slid over every inch of her he could reach. Her nipples were pinched and tugged until he lifted her hands to them and told her to do it. As he moved down her ribs with his hands, he lifted her ass up and watched her every move as he devoured her. Beth came so many times that she lost count, yet he never stopped. And even though she begged him to, many times, she wasn't really sure that she wanted him to.

Her body felt tight and loose at the same, relaxed from all the climaxes, yet ready to bow up to come again when he commanded her to. Or brought her. Nate slid his fingers into her, bringing her so many more times that she finally had to beg him to stop or kill her. When he leaned back from her, telling her not to run, he became the most beautiful wolf she'd ever seen. Then the big animal took her pussy into his mouth.

The wolf, his wolf, fucked her with his tongue as well. But his was longer, rougher than Nate's had been. And when he growled low in his throat, Beth could feel it all over her, as if he'd put a vibrator to her pussy and brought her over again. Beth propped herself up on her elbows when he pulled back again, and Nate stood over her, his lean naked body glistening with a slick dew. She could feel his need was as bad as hers, and she sat up to look at him.

"Take me." He shook his head and fisted his cock. The tip of him was thick and dark with blood. "I want to feel you fuck me. Take me hard. I want to feel you inside of me, deep. Please, Nate. I want you to fuck me."

"No. Lay back. I want to come all over your body." Beth put out her hand, wrapped it around his thick cock, and watched his face as she fisted him as he'd done. He watched her through hooded eyes, his face hard with something so profound that she wanted to see him when he did come. "You're so small. I would hurt you if I made love to you. Please, bring me, love. I need to come in the worst possible way."

Taking him into her mouth, she gagged at his size. When he pulled back and told her to lay down, she felt as if he'd slapped her. She wanted to give him as much pleasure as he had her, and she felt as if she'd done something wrong. But when he held onto the bed post and his hand moved up and down his cock, Beth wanted to feel his cum on her body, needed it like she needed her next breath. The next beat of her heart.

His hand moved up and down his shaft faster and faster, the slickness of his precum making it easier. Beth held her breasts, pulled and tugged at her nipples when he told her to; anything, she thought, to give herself and him some relief. Sliding her fingers down to her pussy, she spread her legs open for him and begged him to give it all to her.

His cum hit her in the face first. It was hot, nearly too much so for her skin. Rubbing it over her body, she cried out as he came on her belly, her breasts, even her mouth. Licking her lips, she took him into her and cried out when he touched his fingers to her pussy again. Beth watched him come on her while his free hand fucked her, making her come twice more. She saw stars, her body felt like it was touched by something electrical, and he wasn't finished with her yet.

"Come for me." She shook her head, begged him once again to take her. "I can't hurt you. Come, Beth. Come for me so that I can watch as you do."

Beth came. She felt her body not just come apart, but shatter into millions of stars, each one of them just behind her eyelids sparkling brightly. And before she could gather her wits, even to breathe, she was coming again, her body no longer just coming apart but back together too hard for her to think that she'd ever be the same. And at that moment, Beth wasn't sure she wanted to be. Not if it involved this man being in her life.

When she opened her eyes, not even realizing that she'd passed out until then, she was alone in the room. She curled to her side, listening to see if he was nearby, and realized he'd left her. Beth found herself depressed, to have shared something so amazing and not to have Nate there to tell him about how she felt, what he'd made her feel like. But then she realized that they hadn't shared, not really. He had not made love to her. He'd come on her, yes, but he'd not given her himself. Nor herself to him.

Getting up, she gathered her tattered clothing and made her way to his shower. Then turning off the water again, she dressed. For some reason she didn't want to bathe in his room, where everything about it smelled of him. Going into the hall, she was surprised at how hard she had to work at not sobbing, and made her way to the lower levels and her room. Beth was glad she met no one coming or going. She had no idea what she might have said had anyone asked her anything.

It took her only a few minutes to get her things gathered up, and she was under the water in her own bath in no time. The tears, ones that had been threatening to fall since she'd left Nate's room, came freely now. As she scrubbed him off her, using the sponge hard enough to tear it in pieces, she thought of what they'd done. What he'd done to her. Or in this case, what he'd not done. Perhaps, her mind thought, she'd not been good enough, worthy enough for the man.

As she turned off the water and stood there, Beth realized that she felt betrayed. No, that wasn't it. She felt unloved, unwanted in a way that tore hard at her heart. A feeling that she'd never felt before, not even from her mom. Getting dressed in her biggest clothing, a sweatshirt and sweat pants, she sat down on the bed, only to get up and start throwing things into her bags. It was well past time that she left anyway.

By the time she'd gathered her things, pitiful amount that there was, she was exhausted. Not just from all the work she'd done, but crying as well, shedding tears for a man that she wasn't going to be able to love. Not because she didn't want to, but because he'd not wanted her to. Her heart hurt as well, not because of what was wrong with it, but from the pain of being so rejected. At some point during her packing, she realized that he hadn't wanted her not because of anything he'd done, but because of what she had wrong with her.

"What man wants to be saddled with a dying girlfriend? Not anyone I know." Which was true. When she'd been diagnosed with her heart condition, her boyfriend of nearly three years had broken it off, saying that while he didn't love her any less, being with her would be such a drag. He'd called her a drag. "Bastard."

When someone knocked on her door, she almost hoped that it was Nate, wondering where she was and how come she'd left him. Well, she didn't really leave him, he'd done that on his own, but she was no longer in his room. Going to the door after debating on it for a few minutes, she asked who was there.

"Skylar. Can I come in?" Beth looked around the room that she'd been given. It was a mess...her bags were on the bed but closed up, and she'd laid out her purse and key to just snatch up and go. "Please? I'd like to talk to you before you leave. You are leaving, aren't you?"

Opening the door, she stared at the beautiful woman. It took her a few minutes of just staring at her to realize what she was seeing. Skylar wasn't human. And if the wings behind her didn't give it away, the tats all over her certainly did.

"Yeah, I get that a lot when someone first comes here." Beth told her she was sorry. "Don't worry about it. The fact that you can now see them answers a lot of questions I might have for you. Nate is down in the gym working off his sexual frustration."

"He wouldn't have to if he'd not left me there all alone." Beth slapped her hand over her mouth, realizing how much she'd said. When Skylar laughed, Beth felt her body heat in embarrassment.

"He's pretty pissed off." Beth just nodded, afraid now to open her mouth. "May I come in? I mean, it's pretty private down here, but I wanted to speak to you."

"I'm just leaving." Skylar nodded. "I can't stay here, not like this. I have things I want to do before I die. And staying here with Nate, I don't think that's going to end very well."

"More than likely not on the path that he's taking with you." Skylar asked again if she could come in. Beth stepped back and Skylar entered. "In the event you haven't figured it out, if you need something while you're here, you have only to think of it. Like a bigger room. A better view. I'm not sure why it works that way—magic, I guess—but it helps when we've so many here. Remy and I are the ones that seemed to be able to give it out; again, not sure how that works, but you need it, it's here for you."

"There are a great many things I want, but I doubt that magic can fix them." Skylar sat down in a chair that hadn't been there before, Beth was sure of it. And when she asked if she wanted something to drink, Beth watched as a pitcher of tea and some scones appeared on a table that also just showed up. Beth sat down. "I don't believe in magic."

"If you didn't, none of this would have been possible. And so you know, I didn't do this, you did. This is your room, and your thoughts are the only ones that can control it. Like I said, Remy and I dole it out, but we don't control what happens in someone's personal space. Like your rooms." Beth nodded, then shook her head. "Think of something but don't say it out loud. I'm betting that it appears before you can finish the thought."

The African violet appeared in a cup in her hand. It was pink too, the most brilliant color she'd ever seen. Setting the cup and saucer on the small table, she looked at Skylar when she handed her a plate of cookies, the plate an exact match to the cup and saucer, as well as a tall glass of tea with the same design etched in it. She wasn't sure what she could say, so said nothing. Beth thought she'd been doing that a lot lately, not having any idea what to say.

With trembling hands, she took the glass to her lips and sipped. She knew that it would be her favorite flavor even before it touched her taste buds. Beth decided that for now she'd keep her thoughts to a minimum. Almost as soon as the thought entered her mind, she knew that it wasn't going to work. All sorts of things popped in there without any kind of order. Like warm socks on her feet. A pillow behind her in the chair. Beth closed her eyes and leaned back, trying to calm her mind.

"You're part of the blood brothers, or the brotherhood. Don't ask me who started calling us that. I'm not sure now, but it fits. The men here, they were called to help first. Then as we all started to arrive, each of them has taken one of the females as a mate. Enhancing them and ourselves as we bonded. Do you know what that means, Beth?" Beth shook her head at Skylar, who nodded. "It's a lot to take in, and trust me when I tell you, it's no easier after you've been here a while. Nate, as you know, was the last of them to take...well, to have his mate arrive. That would be you. Hector, you met him, he said that twelve of us would be needed to complete the magic. At first we thought it was going to be men, all twelve of them. But then he explained that it would be six of each, the men and their mates. But what he didn't count on was—"

"Wait. I don't.... Why do you think I need to know this? Nate has made it very clear that I'm not going to be a part of anything in his life. But just why would there be a need for twelve people to complete the magic? I mean, you seem to have a great deal of it as it is, right? I can see that you all have it in spades, but what does that have to do with me being a part of the twelve? And so you know, I'm not going to be a part of anything. I'm going to be dead before too long." Skylar said nothing but leaned back in the seat. "You can try that 'I so don't care what you think, but you're gonna be here anyway' thing you have down pat, but we both know that I'm not going to be around long."

"Your heart is no longer giving you trouble, is it, Beth? You're healthier now than you've ever been, I'm betting too. I don't want to be indelicate, but I'd bet even though you didn't have intercourse with Nate, you did take a part of him into you." Beth felt her face heat again when she remembered licking him from her lips. "And he would have taken a part of you inside him as well. That's what it would have taken, in the event you didn't know, to make you well again. Though some of it might have been a great deal more enjoyable for you than it was for him, if the way he's beating the bag downstairs is any indication."

"He doesn't want me. And before you say that he does, I've been down this road before. I'm not healthy. The sex might have been really good, but it's not a cure all for what is wrong with me. And even if it was, Nate has made it perfectly clear that he has no more use for me than I do for him. My mouth and what I might have taken into it has nothing to do with my heart issues." Skylar asked her if she was sure. "I'm positive."

"Go see Weston. I'm betting he can tell you that you're perfectly healthy. And that because of your *mouth*, you're also an immortal. I think, and this is just me, the only reason that you've not been marked yet is that you've not completed this bond. With intercourse. At least that's my theory." Beth got up to pace and realized that she did feel pretty good. But she had before when she'd been smart enough to sit down and rest when she needed to. "As I was saying before, what Hector hadn't counted on, nor did he have any knowledge of, was that we'd all come to have more magic than he'd ever given us. Or even dreamed of us having. Recently we've been told it's because of the earth and all the inhabitants here. They wanted us to win this war, and gave us all that they could to make it happen."

"You're saying that Hector gave you magic and some freaky awesome powers, and now you have to come together with all these people to...I have no idea what it is you have to do. But as I have said before, I just don't believe in magic. It's not real. You're all just...I don't know. But it's not magic." Skylar reminded her of the dream she'd had and what she'd said to them when she'd first come here. "A dream, nothing more. I must have heard your names or something, and that's why I knew who you were. I'm not really sure what is going on, but I'm going to leave here before you pull me into your—"

"Do you have a mark on your body? A sword or something?" Beth covered her wrists and stepped back. Beth had no idea how she'd known about the mark that she'd only just found while in the shower, but it had frightened her to no end when she'd cut her finger on the blade when she'd touched it. "You can take it from your body. Just as if it's in the scabbard and you're pulling it out to protect yourself."

75

"No, that's not possible."

Skylar stood up and showed her the one on her ribs, the long sword that looked as if the person who had marked her had been a great artist and had a great deal of talent when he'd marked this woman. When Skylar pulled it from her, by the pummel, Beth watched as she not only held it in her hands, but her wings spread out behind her. Beth felt the floor come up fast, and that was all she remembered.

~~~

Nate felt it…the moment of fear, then nothing. Staggering to the wall where he'd been working out with Leo, he held onto it while he tried to reason with his mind that she was all right, that Beth didn't need him. When he could, he stood up and made his way into the house. Skylar touched his mind then and told him to go to the clinic; that was where she'd taken Beth.

What happened? She was fine, then she was terrified. What did you say to her that made her have to end up in the clinic? Skylar didn't answer him until he entered the clinic where she was. "What did you do to her?"

"*Me?* You'd better take it down a notch or two there, buddy boy, or you'll find yourself laying out there next to her. In a whole lot worse shape, too. I did nothing but try and clean up your mess. What the fuck did you think was going to happen when she woke up in a stranger's bed, naked and alone?" He said nothing, but felt his anger at her double. This was none of her business, and he was on the verge of telling her to back the fuck off when she spoke again. "If you think it'll make you feel better, you go ahead and take that shit out on me. But I'll warn you now, I'm not going to hold back. I'm pretty pissed at you myself."

"I didn't hurt her." Skylar asked him if he was sure about

that. "Yes. When I left her she was sleeping. I thought it best if I let her be so she could. And whatever happened between us is just that. Between us. Not you."

"You abandoned her and ran from the room like a kid who might get caught where he's not supposed to be. I'll ask you again, what the fuck is wrong with you? Did you not think that she'd be upset to find herself alone in your bed?" He said nothing, wondering what Beth had told her. "She told me nothing, you moron. But she was packing when I got to her room."

"Packing? That's not going to happen. What the hell do you think I should do, Skylar? Make love to her and tear her apart? Crush her under my weight? Is that what you're thinking?"

The punch to his face threw him back on his ass, it was so unexpected, and to be honest, quite painful. And before he could get up and.... He wasn't sure what he might have done, but Skylar stood over him and glared down. Nate was terrified in that moment, and he was pretty sure that it was well justified. Skylar was royally pissed off.

"Get up." Being a smart man, he stayed where he was. "I said to get up and fight me, you lousy piece of shit. Get up and try that shit on me if you think you can. Use that weight of yours and try and crush me. I'm pretty sure that I can take it, don't you?"

"You'll hurt me. And if you don't, then Remy will."

Skylar grabbed him by the throat and picked him up, lifting him up over her own height, his weight in this moment meaning not a damned thing. And Nate was afraid that if she threw him, which he had no doubt that she would, that he'd be beyond the magic, and he'd be dead.

"Skylar, honey, what are you doing?" She growled at

Remy when he came up behind her. Nate didn't struggle; in fact, he was sort of afraid to try and get away from her. She'd snap his neck like a twig. "Perhaps we could settle this calmly. Whatever he's done, I'm sure that he's very sorry for it. If you put him down right now, I'm sure that he'd tell you that—"

"Don't humor me, Rembrandt. So help me when I'm finished with this dumbass, I will come after you if you don't back off right now. I'm teaching him a lesson." Nate looked at Remy when he took a step back from her. "What is it you were saying about being too heavy for her? Do you think perhaps you might have overestimated your size when it comes to her? Poor little defenseless female like me has lifted you up without a single problem, haven't I, you dumb shit?"

He was prevented from answering, even if he could have, when one of the motor homes that had been parked by the building started up. Nate looked at Skylar and hoped that she'd let him go. But all she did was give him a hard shake and hold onto him. When the camper was off the grounds, she didn't as much let him down, but did indeed toss him away from her. Before he could get up, she was there again, her blade at his throat.

"You touch her with so much as a bad thought and I will cut your head from your shoulders and dance a jig over the remaining part of you. And if you doubt that I will, you had better have all your ducks in a fucking row before you try." He watched her and felt blood, hot and thick as it ran down his neck, when she pushed the blade into his neck just enough to draw his blood. "She's all that stands between us and Benton. And right now, I think I'd rather he won than you hurt her again. Because you know as well as I do that you did."

"I don't know what to do." She asked him what he wanted to do. "I don't know that either. I won't hurt her, but I know

I will. She's my mate, and as much as I want to take her into my heart, I'm terrified that I'll kill her when I do. The dream, Skylar. I keep seeing her die in my dream, and I don't want to be the one that kills her."

"Think, Nate, think with something besides that dick of yours. Do you suppose there is only one way to have sex? That you must crush her to have it with her?" Nate said nothing. "Christ, do you ever watch porn movies? There are as many ways to have sex as there are men with dicks in this world. Make something up."

"That's not all I'm afraid of hurting her with. I mean, it's not just crushing her." He felt his face heat when she looked at his groin. "I'm not average. I'm not even what one would consider porn star big."

"Oh." He might have laughed if this wasn't so serious. "What have you done about letting her know this?"

"You mean did I whip it out and dance it around for her? No. I didn't." He thought of her face when she'd tried to take him into her mouth. "Now do you understand why this won't work? That fucking Benton took everything away from me."

Skylar dropped her sword and he stood up. When she said nothing, he started past her when she said his name. Nate almost didn't stop; he didn't want to hear that he wasn't going to get another chance at love, that Beth was a wonderful person and he'd figure it out too late. But when he did turn to her, he could see the sorrow on her face and it nearly broke him.

"I'm sorry. I truly am. I never thought...I don't think any of us thought of what happened to you there. Not all of it anyway." He nodded. "If you need anything from me...I'm not sure what it would be, but if you need me, I'm here for you. Forever."

He said nothing, but let his wolf take him. Taking off in the direction that the motor home had gone, he was nearly to it when he felt her fear. Wondering what was going on, he put all the speed that he could into his run, and caught up with her just as she was pulling up in front of a gas station. They'd not turned on the pumps yet, so he stood near one of them and waited for her to get out. When she didn't, he moved to enter and heard the voices before he got the door opened. Somehow her mother had gotten in the motor home before Beth had left, he'd bet anything on that.

"You'll not let him treat me this way, Beth. I'm your mother and I demand that you take my side on this. He thinks I'm harping on him. I've never harped on anyone. And there he is, treating me like some monster when I've done nothing wrong. Nothing, I tell you." Nate smiled when Beth said that she wasn't just harping on her dad, but her as well. "I most certainly am not. But if he would just listen to me and do as I tell him, he'd be better off, you know this. Your father is a mean, vicious person, and as much as I hate to say it, I think there is something wrong with him. In the head. He'd be better off if you'd tell him to—"

"Better off how? By being a doormat to you? I don't think you'd like that any better than if he stood up to you. Which is what I'd tell him to do if he asked my advice." Her mother started sobbing loudly. "That won't work anymore, Mom. I've had it up to here with your whining to me about Dad. There is nothing wrong with him other than he's no longer letting you rule him, like you did me. It's the reason that I left home as soon as I could. I just couldn't take it any longer."

"No one cares how I'm being treated. You all think that I'm just being a horrible person, when all I want is for him to do as I say." Nate shifted and entered the camper just as a loud sob came from Ruth. "I try and try to make us happy, and all he does is snap and treat me poorly. I just don't think anyone knows the things that I have to put up with."

"Yes, we do. You tell anyone and everyone that comes near you what a horrible person Dad is to you. Well, have you thought it might be you that's making him that way?" Her mom stood up and Nate cleared his throat. Ruth looked like she was going to slap her daughter, and one person being hit today was more than enough. Beth turned and looked at him when her mom did. "What are you doing here? I thought you had things to do."

He could hear the hurt in Beth's voice. And the determination. He had to smile...she was very strong when she wanted to be. As he made his way to her and her mom, he was careful where he walked. The little area that served as the living room wasn't big enough for him to be comfortable in. Not without the sides rolled out, and even then, it might have been a little tight.

"I came to talk to you." She said nothing but did lift her chin up. "I was hoping that we could go back to the compound, and you and I could talk about what happened between us."

"Nothing happened between the two of us but that I was a disappointment to you." He started to ask her what she meant by that when her mom sobbed. "Oh, do shut up, Mother. I have enough going on right now without you trying to be the center of attention. Just go back to the compound and stay away from Daddy if he's so mean to you all the time. I'm sure there are any number of places you can go and annoy someone."

"Doesn't anyone care about me anymore? You'd think that I was this bad person, when all I've tried to do is help people when I can and make them see reason. But you'd think, the way that your father and you treat me, I was this horrible person. I'm not." Her mother wailed louder. "Everyone is out to get me and try to make me look bad. I'm not a bad person. I just know that your father isn't the man I married. And you have no idea what I have to endure every day. I try and try, and all I get is grief for my efforts. It's not fair, I tell you. I just want him to listen to me, is that too much to ask?"

Nate had enough. "Sit down and shut the fuck up. And if you so much as open your mouth, I will tie you up, gag you, and bury you in the backyard for the puppies to piss on your head." He turned to Beth. "You, sit over there in the passenger seat and buckle in. I'm taking us back. And we're going to talk about this. Christ, this is a madhouse, and I feel like I'm the only sane person. And that should tell you how fucked up this is. If I was smart I'd put you out here, Ruth, and let the monsters have at you. I've no doubt that they'd lay down their weapons and walk away from you rather than hear you whine. You are by far the most...what is it you want? Him to be your child? It's not going to happen. Now, get over yourself and shut up."

When he had the rig turned around, he put the thing in park and pulled Beth from her seat. Kissing her with all the frustration he had, he held her to him and put her hand over his thick cock. When she started to pant a little, he put her back in her seat and told her to buckle up this time.

He thought of all the ways he could make Beth his mate while he drove them back to safety. This was either going to kill them both or they'd be mates. Either way, he was going to get this thing with her parents taken care of too. By the time he was pulling onto the grounds, it was supper time and late. Nate thought he'd deal with this in the morning.

He turned to the two women, and wasn't surprised to

see that Ruth was pissed. "I would very much like it if you two were to stay apart for the rest of the night. It's late, and everyone's nerves are frayed. In the morning we'll sit down like adults and talk this over. There will be no more trying to leave either, please. It's too dangerous out there with Benton still around."

"I don't like you." Nate just grinned at Ruth. "I'm a grown woman, and I won't have you treating me like I'm a child."

"Perhaps you should think along those terms when you speak to your husband." Nate turned to Beth. "Can we talk for a little while tomorrow sometime? Please? I have something I'd like to explain to you."

At her nod, he felt better and even handed her the keys to her home. When she nodded again and stood up, he did as well. The urge to kiss her, to lay her out on the table and take her, was overwhelming. But when she turned and left the rig, Nate sat down. He'd never been so unnerved in his life as he was thinking about the conversation he needed to have with his mate.

Chapter 6

Master moved as close to the compound as he could get without being seen. They weren't on the grounds this late at night, for which he was glad, but there was no reason for him to be stupid either. It was time to test out a few ideas that he'd had; well, Ward and Dolin had had, but he'd not let on to anyone that they weren't his. Unless of course they didn't work. One of the ideas they'd had was to see how close he could get to the people there when he flew over the compound. To see if at night he could breach the barrier and get into the house where they were at slumber. Taking to the skies, Master had to smile. It was wonderful to feel so good.

Taking flight had never been this easy. He could lift himself up with just a single movement of his wings, and be airborne in less time than he'd been able to do before the water. Even after he'd been changed and Rembrandt had tried to harm him. But he had to do something, and soon, or the water wouldn't be able to keep him feeling so good. Rembrandt, his mind kept telling him. He was to blame for a great many things that had gone wrong.

He was sure now that the water was being taken from him somehow. He'd put out sticks at the water levels several times today, and each time the water had been less, by a great deal. The shoreline was also becoming less lush, like since the water was gone, there was no reason for it to live. The level was going down so fast that he feared the water would be gone before he was able to kill Rembrandt. And that had to happen…he had plans around the other man being dead. For now, however, he had to see how close he could get.

He could almost touch the ground with his wings when he tipped toward it. Master was sure that they'd not thought of him coming at night and were lax in their protection. Flying low again, he could almost taste his victory when he saw the woman in the yard. She stared at him as if she'd never seen such beauty before. Landing near the circle but not close enough to touch it, he looked at her and spread his wings out behind him. Yes, he could tell she was very impressed with him and his strength.

"You will come to me and be my slave." She moved back from him, and he thought about what Ward had told him only this morning. He'd cautioned him about being nicer. That perhaps someone might come to help him if he didn't appear to be so rude all the time. "Please, would you come to me and be my friend? I need one right now. So many of mine have gone on, killed by a murderous fool that I plan to kill soon too."

She didn't back away, and he thought of the other advice that Ward had given him, about being wounded and hurt so that a person might come to his aid. He hated to appear less than he really was, a great creature that was as strong as anyone ever made, but it might work. So far it was, but he didn't have the woman yet so he laid down, trying to look as if he were wounded.

"I know who you are. You're the monster that they talk about all the time." Master smiled. He loved that they talked about him, and he asked her what wonderful things they said. "Nothing so wonderful; more like you're stupid and that you're not going to win this thing you have going against them. They think you're nuts and that you're going to die soon. I'm guessing that they don't care for you overly much."

His temper flared, but Ward told him to tread carefully. He might be able to get some much needed information from this person. He'd said intel, but Master hadn't any idea what that meant until Dolin explained it to him.

"That's not terribly nice, do you think? But I do not care what one says about me, not really. So long as Rembrandt is dead, I know that I am the best there is." She sat down and so did he, curling his wings behind him. "He is the monster in this. Did you know that he killed a dear friend of mine? Ripped the heart from her chest while it still beat. And then he moves about, trying his best to harm me, when I have done nothing but asked him to let me kill him."

"Mary." He nodded, proud that Mary was talked about as well. "I heard that she helped kill Hector's wife, and tried to kill his son too. I don't condone paedocide. Not murder at all, but the murder of a child isn't right." Master didn't know what that word meant, but figured it mattered little in what he wanted.

"She did nothing wrong so far as I can see. Mary was doing what she needed for the betterment of our lives. Killing that woman was a part of a grand plan that was to bring Hector to his knees. Have him do what we needed. But he lied to us by pretending that he had killed himself by hiding away here. That wasn't very fair of him, was it? To be so cruel that he would not help us when we wanted him to? Hector, he betrayed us on more than one occasion after that as well. There were books that he hid away from us, with things in them that we needed, and now he uses that information against me to try and stop me. Why? We were to kill him first, not him get away before we had finished our use of him. And that child was to die to get Hector to do as he was told to. But as far as I can see, he lived, so there was no reason for them to kill Mary. While most of the time I don't like her overly much, she was a good woman who was needed to make things work for us." She pointed out that Dolin and Ward had not just killed Hector's wife, but a great many other people as well. "As I have said, they were necessary to the cause. Can you not see that? They killed Mary for no reason other than to have her dead. What sort of monster does that? Had they just died as they were told then things would have gone well for us. We would all be rich beyond anyone else, ruling you as it should be. I am going to be master soon, and when I am, you shall see how things should have been from the start."

"You mean you would have gotten what you wanted, and to hell with everyone else." He nodded, not sure why she sounded as if this wasn't the correct order of things. He was Master, after all. "I see. My mom is a great deal like you, I think. Selfish to the point that she cares nothing for others around her or how she makes them feel. Harping about how things should be the way she wants them simply because she says so. And as long as she is right and everyone is paying attention to her, then things are calm for a little while. At least until she finds that people no longer are in her circle of drama, or have gone on to do as they please. Which to my way of thinking is the way it should be. My mom likes to be in control, and to hell with your feelings on the matter."

"Feelings. Humans are so hung up on feelings. I should think that you'd be over that by now. They're messy, as well as false. No one has true feelings now. Just look at you. You have pretended to be my friend, yet you have not come to me as I have asked. And I was even polite about it too. Just as Dolin and Ward suggested." She told him that she wasn't his friend and doubted she ever would be. "Honestly, I do not care if you are or not, but you will do as you are told when I rule. If not, then you will die with all of the rest."

"No. I don't think you'll rule at all. And as for feelings, I think you're wrong about that too. Some of them are very nice. As for pretending to be your friend, I think you're stuck where you are, the same as me, and you are lonely. Anyone standing out here would have been someone for you to talk to. And to try and get you what you wanted. You said you wished for me to be your slave. Well, fuck that crap. I'm not a slave to anyone." He wanted to roar out to her that she wasn't playing fairly, but he saw the man before he could. She turned to the man when Master stood up and spread his wings. When she turned her back to him, something that vexed him terribly, he wanted to cross the barrier and kill her for her treatment of him. The woman spoke to the man then. "He's just telling me what a friend he is to me. I think he's only trying to butter me up so he can get me to do something for him. A lot like other people I know."

"Benton? What are you doing here? We actually thought you'd done us all a favor and died. I guess I owe Remy ten bucks. He said you were too stupid to do as you should." He tried to hold his temper and tell the man he was Master, but he laughed and Master told him to shut up. "You don't like to be called by your given name, is that it? Well, that's too fucking bad. And as you've been told before, you're not master to any of us."

"I will be, and soon." Master wanted to kill this man almost as much as he did Rembrandt. To bring him to heel and make him beg for mercy before he tore him in half. Master thought of his newfound strength, the way he was stronger than any of them, but Ward told him to wait…it would do him no good to show himself now. It was tempting to test his powers and kill them both. But Ward was right, he would not show his strength just yet. Master knew now that there were others out here, the man and the woman, that the dome over the compound would be in place. He'd have to come back when they were all abed and attack them while they rested. "When I come back here, you will rue the day that you have not done as you were told and given me my due."

"When you come back here, you can bet I'm going to give you what I think you're due. Right before I piss on your remains." Master blew his fire over the couple, and he wanted to stomp his feet when nothing happened to them. His flames blew up and over them as if they were shielded. Master tried twice more before he felt his anger start to rise up and some of the blackness that still plagued him took over. After several moments of just glaring at the couple he had control of himself again. Moving back into the wooded area, wishing now that he'd not stopped to talk to the woman, he tried to think if they'd given him any information that he could use. Nothing. Not even enough for him to know who the man and woman were.

"I'll get that too, just before I'm set to kill them." He was back to his lair when he remembered that he'd forgotten to try flying over the compound again. "Women are the ruination of all my plans. Everyone one of them. Had she only done what I told her to do, then I would have killed her and been able to test things out. But she distracted me, just as she was made to do."

Master was weaker than before he'd left. The encounter and his anger had drained him. Sitting down on his stone, using his flame to light the circle that he'd been using to keep warm, he tried to think why he'd be so exhausted. It had been only a short walk and a little flying around.

He'd not been able to eat for days, that was it. Not that there wasn't plenty of game around, but he'd not been hungry. His body was still fit, so it bothered him little, but he thought that at some point he might need to feed his belly. Setting flame to his walls to warm the cave, he sat down and looked at the walls where his drawings were; his plan, which he'd thought of with very little help from Ward and Dolin.

The plan was perfect and he knew it. Ward and Dolin both had even told him that he was very good at this part, and if he could do but only half of what he'd planned, then he would defeat Rembrandt and rule. He had told them that he knew this, but was glad to hear it from someone so close to him.

"The first thing I plan to do is to crush his women. I know that it is secondary on my list, but I shall move it to the first position when it is time." Ward, ever present, now asked him why he'd do that. "Because I do not like them. Women are... well, I believe them to have the ear of men and get them into trouble. A great deal of trouble, as a matter of fact. If I should kill them secondly, after the men are dead or jailed, they will go to find another man to suck dry, and soon all men are going to be useless to me. Then who will I have to rule? I shall put a stop to them."

He wasn't entirely sure how he was going to bring that about. Master knew enough about the human race to understand that women were a necessary evil, but he didn't have to like them. He would pick the few that he would need to repopulate the world for him to have slaves, then the rest would have to die. That way there would be less problems in his new world.

"They'll feel privileged that I have chosen them to do this special thing, to give me more slaves. I will make them have sex with only the healthiest of men too. That way they will be strong of back, but I shall curb their learning. I do not want them to be smart as well as strong. The rest, the ones that must die? They will know that their bloodline was inferior to my needs, and go with a heavy heart to their deaths. Perhaps some will not enjoy this, but they'll understand in the end, and perhaps feel like they have gone on for the betterment of my world."

Master closed his eyes after lying down. He would need to rest the day away, for tonight he was going to go and kill Rembrandt. It was well past time to get things finished between him and the man.

~~~

Ruth sat at the table and tried to get her thoughts in order. Last night Bethany had asked her to make a list of what she felt like was wrong with her father, and he was to do the same. Ruth knew that he'd have trouble with his list...there wasn't anything she was doing that he'd have to write down. But when she offered to help him, he'd gone to another room and didn't speak to her. She added his stubbornness to ask for help to her mental list.

When Nate came into the room, she asked him if he'd go and talk to Lyle, as she'd politely asked him to do several times in the last twenty-four hours. Someone needed to, and this big man might be able to get through to him. She told him that if he had to use a heavy hand on her husband, then that would be all right too, so long as Lyle would listen to her when she told him how things needed to go. But when Nate lifted his hand, as if to cut her off, she bit her lip. Some people were just rude. But she'd wait...she wasn't going to stoop to his level of meanness to get him to help her out.

"I've yet to have my breakfast, and I'm in a foul mood. So unless you want to hear me curse, then I would suggest you hold off for a while. You will not like what I have to say to you. I'm going to have a long talk with Beth today to settle a lot of things. So, with me being in a crappy mood because of you being all over me and lack of sleep, I'd back off for now." She tisked at him and started to get up to get him some toast. It's what she was having, and that would get him in a better mood. But almost as soon as he sat down, there were three large platters of food put in front of him by Ann.

"You cannot seriously be thinking of eating all of that. Let me take some of that and store it away for—" He slapped her hand away from the food. "Well, I never. What is wrong with you? I was only trying to help you. Do you want to get fat? I'll take that now, and you'll thank me for it later."

"What I want is for you to leave me alone. This is what I eat. In the event that you didn't notice, I'm a big man with a huge appetite. Now, you touch my food again and I will snap your arm off and beat you to death with it. I told you, I need to eat and I'm in a bad mood." Ruth reached again for his plate and he growled at her. Actually growled like some kind of animal. "Get away from me."

"I don't think you understand that eating like that will make you overweight. Men need someone to watch over them. And if you won't see reason, then someone will have to do it for you." Reaching for the plate again, knowing that he'd not be able to eat all of that, the snapping of his teeth at her arm startled her. "What is wrong with you? I'm sure once you think this over, you'll see that I'm right. That is entirely too much food for one person. If you would just let me have my way...why is it men are forever thinking that they know better?"

"I'd back off now, miss. Unless you want him to show you his other self." Ruth looked at Ann when she laid several more slices of bacon on his already overflowing plate. "Nate eats like this every day. You'd best just keep your mouth shut and your hands back, or he'd be biting you. I don't think you'd like that much."

"He will not change into an animal. I'll be upset if he does. And you're not helping him, Ann, by giving him what he wants. You're actually harming him. When breakfast is over, you and I will sit down and have a long conversation about calories and healthy eating. I'm sure that no one has taught that to you where you come from. You'll feel better too once you are on a good diet of the kind of food I'll tell you about." She looked at Nate. "I think you're just doing this to upset me. I don't understand why it is that you think I need anyone upsetting me more. You're just being cruel. Like Lyle is."

"You're forever saying that people are cruel to you, or that someone is mean to you. If you ask me, I think you bring all of this on yourself. If you would just shut the fuck up, as I have told you to do several times, I think you'd see that you're about ninety-nine percent of the problem. Lyle is a good man. And had I been married to you? Well, let's just say that you'd not be treating me the way you do him. I'd have left your ass on the side of the road." Ruth drew back her hand to slap him and he smiled at her. "Do it, and I swear to you that they won't get you to the clinic fast enough when I finish with you. Because trust me when I tell you, the moment your hand touches my face, you're as good as dead. I've had enough of your advice and whininess."

"Nate? Mom?" Ruth looked at Bethany and started to tell her what this man was doing to her. But her own daughter cut her off before she could so much as explain how mean he was to her. "Will you please just leave him alone? Or is it your plan to alienate every person you come in contact with from now on? Christ, you're like a dog with a bone about making people see what a victim you are, when all you are is a bully."

Ruth was shocked. Her own daughter was turning against her? Lyle had done this. Or this man in front of her. She watched him carefully, waiting for the perfect time to take the food. She knew as well as he did that he wasn't going to finish that all, and she wasn't going to allow him to waste it.

Before she could make good on her need to take care of Nate, her husband walked in the door. He was going to listen to her as well. Ruth had always prided herself on knowing what was best for people, and the sooner they all figured out that she really only had their best interests at heart, they'd be a good deal nicer to her. And listen to her.

"Did you take your meds? And those are not the things that I laid out for you, Lyle. I wanted you to wear a tie and the blue suit today when we went house hunting." He didn't say anything to her, but smiled at Ann when she handed him a glass of tea. "Lyle, go back to our room and put on the things I laid out for you. I swear to you that you'd wear whatever you could put your hands on if it wasn't for me. And don't think I didn't notice that you're not answering me about your medications. What would you do if I were not here to remind you all the time? I swear, you'd be dead or in the hospital somewhere."

"I'm not going house hunting with you today. And you're right about my choices of attire. I'm not putting on a tie, nor am I wearing a suit. I'm on vacation. A vacation that you made me take when I was perfectly happy to stay at home and tinker on my projects." She huffed at him and got up to go get the things that he should be wearing. "If you're going to get the tie and other things, I threw them out. And if you ask again, yes, I took my meds. Like I do every day before you ask me. You should know, too, that I'd not have to be taking medications if you weren't around to drive me bat shit every second of every day."

"She asks you every day? Why, if you already take them?" He told Nate that she wouldn't stop. When Nate looked at her, Ruth lifted her chin. Did these people not see that Lyle was not right in the head and that he needed her to remind him of things? "Why on earth would you hound a man over something that he does without you reminding him? Why don't you just leave the poor man alone?"

"I do not hound. And he needs me to remind him or he'd not take them. But you'll go and change now, Lyle. I'll not have you looking like a hobo when we're out and about. And if you have indeed thrown out that blue suit, you'll have to wear the brown one I packed for you. We have to be in public today, and you'll dress the part of being with me." She eyed the nearly empty plates in front of Nate. "You're not a nice person either, are you? And if you think that I'm going to allow you to date my daughter, well, you just get that notion out of your head right now. She's coming to live with us, and selling that monster of a motor home. When she's better, then I'll help her find herself someone to date. A person that she can be proud of."

"First of all, Mother, I will do as I please when I please. And if you think I'd ever live with you again, then you are as nutty as I already think you are. Secondly, he's never asked me to date him, and if he did, that would be between the two of us, and not you." Bethany sat down at the table when Lyle did and asked Nate for a slice of bacon, which he gave her three. "Thirdly, and most importantly, you should know that I'm going to keep my motor home and travel anywhere you're not. You're not going to be riding with me. I'm not going to allow you to call me every ten seconds, and you most certainly will not be trying to tell me what to do. I, too, am a grown woman. You know what, Mom? I never realized what a bully you are."

Ruth started to cry. Everyone was so mean to her of late. And she'd done nothing wrong. If she wasn't here for them, all would go to ruin, and they just didn't realize how much she'd suffered in silence to make things work. When she was handed a tissue, she looked up at Lyle, and before she could tell him that she just wanted the best and that he'd have it if he'd just listen to her when she told him what to do, he spoke.

"I'm fed up with your ways, Ruth. Seriously fed up with them. If you don't back off, I'm going to have to leave you. You've already driven Beth away with the way you nag and push people in the direction that you think we should go." He leaned back against the counter when she stood up. "I do wonder whatever you'll do if you don't have someone to make miserable. But it won't be me. Not anymore. I'm going to fight you at every turn to become a man I can be proud of, not the whipping post of some harpy that I used to love."

"Lyle, I can't believe that you're talking to me this way." She looked at the rest of the people in the room. "Do you see what I have to put up with? Lyle needs me to keep him straight and his life in order. If it wasn't for me he'd not take his medicines, nor would he dress himself properly. What would happen to him then? Do you think it's easy for me to take his treatment and stay this chipper all the time? No it is not. I think there is something wrong with him. I need someone to be on my side with this and make him listen to me."

97

"Chipper? Not a word I'd use to describe you, that's for sure. And for the record, I take my meds without your constant harping on me. I have never once left the house naked, and even if I did, no one would care. We can't socialize with the neighbors because you have hounded them to death and made enemies of every one of them. Even to the point that some have left their home so as not to have to put up with you." Lyle looked at Nate and spoke to him. "She goes around the neighborhood telling them when they can take down their decorations or put them up. Not only that, but she has even gone so far as to paint houses that aren't a color she approves of. Can you believe that? Like it's any of her damned business. And if she thinks that their decorations or yard ornaments are too gaudy or too out of character for the person that lived in the house before them, she writes them this long letter and sticks it on the broken down decorations that she'd not approved of. Decorations that she herself had destroyed in the name of getting things to be her way. Twice we've had to pay for things that she has deemed inappropriate, and then there are countless other things that she's done that resulted in restraining orders for her not to enter properties on our own fucking street."

"Do they want their house to look like a garage sale? I think not. And if they can't see what they're doing to our neighborhood and the value of all our houses, then I don't understand. Why would anyone get upset with a little advice, I ask you? I just want things to look nice." She huffed. "One year this woman had put out an entire grave yard at Halloween a full week before that wretched holiday. Complete with names on the headstones and ghost like things hanging from the trees. Do you know what happened when I asked her nicely to take them down? She put up more. I can't have her doing things like that. It's not the way that things are done."

"Why not?" Ruth looked at Nate when he spoke. "Why is it any of your business what someone does in their own yard? Were you paying her taxes? Making her house payment? If not, then you should have stayed in your own yard and left hers alone. I'm sure the kids trick or treating would have loved it. As for the rest, I'd have brought you up on charges and made sure you were run out of town…tarred and feathered too."

"She called the cops on the kids that used to ride their bikes up and down the streets." Everyone turned to her when Lyle spoke. "She's called them so many times to say that they were vandalizing our yard, which they weren't, that now no one comes on our street unless they have to. And most of the neighbors have put up tall fences so that they can go into their yards without her telling them that they can't do this or that. Another thing that she's made everyone upset about is the way they shovel their drives, where they put out their trash cans on collection day, anything and everything that she can get her two cents in for. Not even at Christmas time when all the lights are up. We used to have people drive for miles just to see the way our street was done up for the holiday. Now no one even bothers because of her. I've had to pay for so many damaged strings of lights that I can't even begin to put a monetary value on them."

"I asked them to put up a single color. Not those flashing ones either. Out of respect for someone that has lived there for so long. I should know how things were in the past, don't you think? But oh no, everyone put up every color in the world, and not tastefully like I asked. I suggested—nicely too, no matter what they say—that they only put them on the roofs and candles in the window if they wanted. No trees should have been in the yard. What were they going to do, have their party out of doors? Our street looked like we were a red light district somewhere." Crying harder now that they were bringing up things that simply had nothing to do with her, she wiped her nose as she continued. "If everyone would just do as I suggest, then I wouldn't have to resort to harming their things so they'll understand. I know what's best, and I want everyone to follow the rules. Without rules there is no order. And there has to be order. If not, then how will things look nice?"

"Your rules, you mean. The rules that you've set up on that dark mind of yours. You want people to do as you say or else feel your wrath. Is that right?" She looked at Nate when he spoke. "You want everyone to follow your rules or you make them pay. Or sometimes, Lyle has to pay. Is that it? You have to be in charge and have it your way, or it's just wrong?"

"I don't understand what you're saying to me. Of course things would be better if they listened to me. But I can't make them, can I? My own husband doesn't listen to me when I try and make him do the right thing. Just look at the way he's dressed. Doesn't that make you see what I have to deal with? How he never bothers with the things I need for him to do?" She took a step back when he stood up. "You have no idea what I have to put up with all day. He's terribly mean to me."

"I think you bring that on yourself by making unrealistic demands on people that you should just leave alone. Do you have your list?" She was confused for a moment. "The list that Beth asked you to make up."

"I didn't write it down if that's what you're asking for. I saw no need for me to point out all of Lyle's problems. We'd be here all day should I do that. Most of them I'm working on, so there wasn't any need for me to air them out in public."

Nate only laughed at her. "I suppose you helped him with his list? He certainly wouldn't have been able to find things to add to it without someone filling his ear with lies and things that aren't right. I bet that you and he got together, and you pointed out every flaw you think I have."

"No. I'm sure his list would pretty much cover all your flaws all on his own. It's small wonder that the man doesn't have a cramp in his hand. Or for that matter, enough paper to list them all." She didn't know how he'd have any to put on his list other than she cared too much, and said as much to him. "Yes, I do believe that you think that would be true. But I've spent the last hour with you, and I've come to realize that you really are a bully, as Beth said. If you're not in control, then it's going to be trouble for those that would dare to disagree with you. And you're a malicious woman who would hurt others rather than see their ways. Because it's all your way or no way at all, correct?"

"You make me sound like I'm a tyrant. I'm not. I'm a caring, loving person. Some people can't see that because they're so set to make me feel bad about helping them. I like to be helpful. It's what I do best." Nate said nothing. "I don't understand you. I think you're just as cruel, if not more so, than Lyle is. And I'm not sure, but I don't think I like you very much either."

"I really don't give a flying fuck if you do or not. But the fact remains that you're not happy unless things are going your way." He looked at Bethany and Ruth stepped between them. "That is a good way to get set aside, willingly or not. I want to talk to Beth, and you're not going to be standing between her and I when I do. Now please move, or I shall have to force you to."

She stood her ground with this man. If she didn't show

him that she wasn't going to let him run over her, then he would for as long as they were here. But instead of giving way to her as people did all the time when they saw reason, he moved around her and took Bethany into his arms. Ruth was so shocked by that she had to count to ten before she could speak. But before she could gather her thoughts on how to deal with this man, he spoke to Beth in a voice that made her think there was more going on between them than there should have been.

"I was wondering if I could have a word with you. It won't take long, but I want to explain something to you." Ruth tried again to move between them, but short of knocking her daughter away, there wasn't any room for her to get between them. Without even looking at her, Nate spoke again, this time his voice was hard and unforgiving. "Ruth, I swear to Christ, I'm going to tie you to a chair. This does not concern you in the least. Behave yourself or you're not going to like me at all."

"You'll stay away from my daughter. She's not going to date you. I've told you this before." Bethany told Nate that she'd go with him, anywhere but here. "I'm coming as well. Whatever you have to say to her, you can tell us all. I don't know what you think your plans are concerning my daughter, but you will not be doing things to her without my permission. Do you hear me, young man?"

"Mother, if you so much as leave this room in the next ten minutes, I will disappear. And you know that I can, I've done it before when you decided to ruin my life." Ruth took a step back from Bethany. That hadn't been her fault either, but every time Beth was mad, she'd bring up that incident again and again.

"I did that to save you. You know that job would never

have satisfied you the way you thought it would. And I didn't do anything that any mother wouldn't do." Bethany said nothing. "I only told that man that you'd been in prison to keep you from taking that job. Do you know how far away you would have been from me? You should be thanking me for doing that, not condemning me every time you get a little upset with me."

"You told him that I was a liar and a thief. You called up my boss, at the job that I wanted since I'd been in high school, and lied to him. And by the time I'd found out and was able to fix it, he'd hired someone else for the position. All because of you." Ruth said it was the best thing for her. "No, Mother, it was the best thing for you. Not me. You ruined it for me. And in turn made it hard for me to ever trust you again. Stay here. I don't want you coming with me, or so help me, you'll regret it. For as long as I live, you'll regret it."

Ruth was standing in the kitchen alone but for the cook, Ann. When she told her to sit, that it was time they went over the daily menus, Ann told her to go to hell. Then Ruth burst into tears. No one was doing what she wanted, and she didn't understand how they thought it was going to work if she didn't help them.

Chapter 7

Nate tried to think how he was going to do this. He either had to talk to her now or Skylar was going to. And as much as he respected the other woman, he was pretty sure that she'd hurt him if she had to. She had already broken his nose. Then later, after he'd returned from bringing her and her mom back to the compound, Skylar had hunted him down for a talk.

"What is it you hope to accomplish with Beth?" He asked her what she meant. "Well, you're not sleeping with her. She still has her own rooms. What is it you think is going to happen when Benton comes here and she's not your mate?"

"I don't want to hurt her." Skylar had cocked a brow at him. "Why do I have to keep pointing out to you how much larger I am than a normal man? Even lying with her, I'm terrified of crushing her. Then there is the added fear of sex. She'd be hurt if I take her."

"You think that you're the only man in the world with a big dick? You're not. I'd say you're just a chicken shit, and this is a fine excuse for you not to be happy."

He growled at her. In hindsight, he probably should have thought before he did that. She was strong and had more magic than he did by a great deal. And he also knew that she was short tempered when it came to the people in the compound, and when they were mistreated she always fought for the underdog. And to her, Beth was the underdog.

The fist to his face again had knocked him back in the chair. And before he could get up, even if he thought that might have been a good idea, she had her sword at his neck and piercing his skin just enough that he knew she meant business. Nate thought for a fallback way to make someone listen to her, she was good at this.

"Now. I'm going to tell you something and you're going to think very hard before you speak. Understand?" He said that he did. "Good boy. Did you know that Beth came to talk to me? Well, I'm sure that wasn't her plan, but I saw her and I got her to talk to me. She thinks you're avoiding her because she isn't pretty. Or for that matter, up to your standards. I tried to tell her that you have no standards at all, because a man like you should be grateful that anyone even spoke to you, but she didn't think that was right either."

"I think she's beautiful." Skylar asked him when he'd told her that. "Well, never. But I was getting around to it. We seem to have people around when I see her, and I'll tell her when the timing is right."

"No you won't, and you know it. And don't lie to me. I can read you like a book." He said nothing. "Okay. I want you to understand that while you're a pain in the ass most of the time, I like you. You're a good man, most of the time, and you seem to...well, you used to have your head out of your ass. But with her, you have lost all your marbles. Do you need help picking them up?"

"If you mean to ask me if I need help with Beth, then I guess you think I do." The blade went a little deeper. "That fucking hurts, damn it. And I don't know what to say to her. Christ, how do you tell a woman that you'd like to fuck her hard enough to move mountains, but you are terrified that while you're at it, you'll tear her up inside?"

She grinned at him. "That, my dear friend, is exactly how you do it. Honesty is the best in this. Let her decide if you're too much for her. And while you're at it, you should get her a dozen or so roses, as well as some chocolate. I understand from her dad that she enjoys both."

So here he was taking her to his room to talk to her, and he was pretty sure that she was going to be pissed at him. Or run screaming into the night. Opening the door, he let her go in first. He might have gone a little overboard on the flowers and chocolate, but he'd had fun, and Whey had helped him.

"Oh my goodness. Oh my goodness, they're beautiful. And so many." She went to the first few vases and smelled the flowers there. He'd not gone with just roses, but any kind of flower that Whey could find. Roses and daffodils. There were daisies and violets too. He had vases of carnations and sunflowers. When she stopped by the table full of boxes of chocolates, he moved to stand next to her. Yes, he supposed that five dozen boxes of different kinds of chocolate had been a bit much, but he liked it too, and thought she might want to share. Now he just felt stupid.

"I wasn't sure what sort you liked, so I got them all." He picked up one of the candy bars that were scattered around the boxes of all sorts of shapes and colors and opened it. He offered her half. "When I found out that you liked them, I really had an idea to get you a box and share it with you. But I found that a candy bar, something that I rarely ate before this, is pretty good. And I'd never had dark chocolate before. Who knew something so bitter could be so satisfying? So I got all I could find of those too. So you know, the closet is stuffed with more of the stuff for you."

"I love all chocolate, in any form and flavor. Dark has

to be my favorite, but I can eat the milk chocolate kind like there's no end to it." She munched on the half he'd given her and took two more before sitting on the edge of the bed. "I'm assuming that this is leading up to something."

"I'm a big man." She nodded, and he got embarrassed. "I mean, you've seen me. My cock isn't normal. And for as much as I'd love to make love to you, I don't want you to be hurt."

"So you left me alone because you're afraid that your big cock will be too much for me." He nodded. "Are you always this selfish? Or is it just me?"

"Selfish? No. I don't...why am I being selfish?" She stood up and began unbuttoning her blouse, then tossed it over to the bed. He nearly swallowed his tongue when she took off her pants and panties all in one movement. Nate was distracted for a moment, but closed his eyes and counted to ten before starting to talk to her again. "I just wanted to explain to you. You know, the reason that we can't have sex. Not the normal way anyway. I can't hurt you, and I would...what are you doing?"

"I'm undressing. And no, you can't hurt me. But I think that the size of your cock is wonderful. I've thought about it a great deal too. How it would feel inside of me." Nate adjusted his cock and she put her hand over him. He felt the heat of her touch all the way to his head and through his balls. "You're very full. And long. I think that feeling you take me will be something to get used to, but unlike you, I'm willing to try."

He moaned when she cupped him in her hot hand. He leaned into her touch, and nearly fell over when she tightened her grip on him. "Aren't you afraid that I'll tear you up?" His voice didn't sound like his own, but he asked her again when she didn't answer him. As she worked the zipper down over him, he moaned when she slipped her hand into his boxers

108

and touched his cock. "You're making me harder. And needy. I want to come so badly that I ache with it."

"Good. I'm going to take you into my mouth now, and you're not going to pull back. Understand?" He nodded, not sure this was a good idea. When she dropped to her knees in front of him, all he could think about was being careful. When he was free of his pants, Nate cried out when she wrapped her hand around him. "I love the way you feel. Hard and slick. And the way that my hand doesn't fit around you makes me so wet that I can feel it on my thighs."

He wasn't sure he could speak right now, so he just watched her. Nate was positive she was going to tell him no way, that he really was too much for her. But when her tongue wrapped around his crown, he reached out for something to hold onto and it just happened to be her head.

Her mouth was warm, wet, and her tongue danced over him so much that he was dizzy with it. Fingers touched his balls, and she cupped them in her hands. Nate fucked her gently, moved in and out of her mouth as slowly as he could, but she was making him crazy with the need to pound her, and he had to pull her back.

"I need to come." She nodded and put her mouth over his cock again. "Please, baby, let me come all over you again." Beth let him go with a little pop and grinned at him.

"Come in my pussy, Nate. Fuck me." He shook his head. "Then you get nothing else from me."

He burned with the need to come. Picking her up to fuck her, he growled at her when she wrapped her legs around him. His need was out of control. His balls hurt, his cock burned. When her legs opened up, he could smell her pussy and it made him insane to have her. Filling her quickly, slamming deep inside of her, he stopped moving when she screamed.

"Again." He looked at her face. "Christ, fuck me before I die. Fuck me, Nate. I need to come like that again."

The wall behind her shook when he pressed her hard against it. He couldn't have stopped now if someone had put a gun to his head. She was his, his mate, and he was going to show her. As he took her, his mouth moved over her neck and face as he tasted every part of her he could. When she came again, screaming out his name, he didn't stop but pounded her again and again as he licked the pounding pulse at her throat. When she held him to her, Nate felt his balls curl up, ready to release, when she bit down on his shoulder. Nate sank his teeth deep into her throat and tasted her blood just as he came.

Every part of him seemed to empty in that second. Then as he continued to fuck her, take her harder and harder as he did so, his balls filled again. His cock stretched deeper into her, as if seeking a spot that would bring them both to completion. And when she lifted her breast up to him, seemingly feeding him, he bit down hard enough to drink from her as she curled her hands into his hair and held him to her.

His body wasn't his own; Nate was mindless to how hard he was taking her. How much of her blood he was drinking. When she lifted his head up by his hair, he stared at her. Nate was worried that he'd hurt her. That was when he realized that he was still fucking her, slowly yes, but still moving in and out of her.

"You're amazing." He grinned, telling her that she was pretty amazing herself. "You're going to make me come again if you keep that up."

"Would that be so bad?" He moved harder, deeper inside of her, punching his cock into her just a little deeper each time. "You're so tight around me. Christ, it's all I can do not to come again and again. You came that first time and I thought I'd hurt you."

"You did a little, but feeling you there, filling me up, was all I could think about. That was well worth a little pain." He lifted her breast up again and thumbed her nipple. "I've never enjoyed sex this much before. It's like I've been waiting just for you to give me such pleasure."

"I can give you more." She nodded and he leaned down to her breast and bit into just her nipple this time. Suckling on her until she began to move faster under him, he looked up at her when he cupped her ass in his hand and pulled her tighter. "Do you have any idea how terrified I was of you?"

"Yes. You were avoiding me—oh yes, more." He fucked her by rolling his hips, moving his groin against her clit until she screamed again. "You should take me to the bed and let's see if that works too."

He tensed up and she put her hands on either side of his face and looked deeply into his eyes. Nate had no idea if she could see into him, but before he could tell her that he was worried again, she bowed up from the wall and screamed. His own pain alerted him to the fact that they were evolving, that she wasn't coming again. Then darkness, a complete and utter darkness, seemed to simply swallow him up.

~~~

Beth started to move, just to get into a better position on her bed, when someone put their arm around her and pulled her closer to their body. The soft snore had her look to her right, and she remembered what had happened. She'd had sex with the most wonderful man, and then the pain had started.

Lifting her arm, she looked at the markings there. For some reason it didn't surprise her that she was marked up like the others in the house. Skylar and the rest of the women in

111

the group had told her that it would happen someday, that it was incredibly painful, and afterwards, she'd have magic. She wasn't ready to believe in the magic part just yet, but so far they'd been dead on with all the rest of what would happen to her.

"You will have marks all over you. I can't read them, but if you want, you can ask Ryiah. She's who we go to when we need to. Her and Rick can read them now." Beth looked over at Nate when he spoke to her. His voice was soft, almost like a caress over her skin and heart. "I should have told you. I'm sorry."

"Skylar did." He nodded and rolled to his back. It was as natural to her as breathing to lay her head on his chest, her body over his. His heart was beating slow and steady, and she closed her eyes when it relaxed her. "What happens now? I mean, to us."

"What would you like to happen? If you want to know the truth, I haven't been able to think beyond how lovely you are and how much I've fallen in love with you." She looked up at him and he smiled. "You made it very easy to fall in love with you. And now that we're officially a couple, I'd very much like for you to move in here with me. Please?"

"I was dying a week ago. No hope for anything. Now here I am, and not only is my heart no longer killing me, but it's so full of you that it's hard to imagine being without you. How is that even possible?" He kissed her on the forehead. "That is not an answer."

"No, but it works." Beth pinched him on the nipple. "Not fair. Okay. The heart being repaired was your first question. My cum, when you took me into your mouth the other day, did that. And some magic too that is in abundance all around here, I guess. I'm not sure what all played a part in this, but mostly my seed would have healed you. Falling in love is easier. I'm a shifter. And the animals that I have in me, for the most part, are like all of their counterparts. Find a mate, fall in love, and breed. Not very sexy, I guess, but that is the way that the kingdom works. I think I would have fallen in love with you this quickly even without being a paranormal. You're wonderfully beautiful. Intelligent. Funny and loving. A little on the bossy side, but I don't care about that if you continue to make me come like you did."

Beth decided to ignore the bossy part. She wasn't, she was pretty sure, but she had worked hard all her life not to be her mother. In the future, she'd be very careful of not laying out his clothing. Not that she thought he'd wear them any more than her dad did, but that wasn't going to be her. Changing the subject, she laid her head down only to lift it again when he rocked into her.

"Stop that. We're having a conversation. Now. The other stuff...the marks? What do they mean? Not what do they say, but why do we have them?" He lifted her arm and put his against hers. They were the same. His were darker than hers were, most of them were wider in places, but they were the same all the way down to the back of her hand. "How do you get around other people when we're marked this way?"

"Humans can't see them. Or so we've only just discovered." She put her arm down and rolled to sit across his groin. His cock was stiff, and she fisted him while she rode him. "If you keep that up, I'm going to come on you again, or you can take me inside of you and we can both enjoy this."

He helped her settle over him, holding his cock in his hand as she lowered her body over his. Christ, he was thick, and she felt herself come quickly when she was sitting on him. He was deeper this way, his cock feeling like it was right at the back of her throat. And she had to be careful too. When she moved over him too quickly, she would nearly unseat herself, and that wasn't good. Riding him slowly, getting used to being able to control things, she thought about all the things she wanted to do to him.

"When you're there, beautifully displayed over me, all I can think about is coming. Do you have any idea how gorgeous you are?" She shook her head and cupped her breast in her hands. "Tug on your nipples for me. Make them hard as stone and I'll feed from them. Nursing from them like that, you make my balls so tight that I can hardly think."

"You bit me here before." She pulled on her nipple and felt it all the way to her pussy. "Riding you is giving me all sorts of ideas. Like sucking on your nipples too. Do you think I could bite you there?"

"Yes. And I'd love it if you did." Leaning down, she took the morsel into her mouth and sucked hard. He lifted his hips up when she bit down, fucking her as she took her pleasure from him. And when she bit down hard enough to draw blood, she cried out when a climax took her breath away. "More. Come on me more."

She came twice more before he rolled them to the side. When he took her to her back, his cock still inside of her, she could tell that he was being careful of her. He was thinking more of not hurting her than he was taking any pleasure. He was a big man, but she wasn't a weakling either. Wrapping her feet over his calves, she rose up with every one of his strokes until he was taking her just the way she wanted. When she came again, crying out his name, he offered her his throat and Beth felt her teeth shift in her mouth, her eye teeth stretch, and she was hungry. For him. Beth bit him like he had her, licking the pulse at his throat then sinking her teeth into his flesh.

Blood filled her mouth. It wasn't coppery tasting like she'd thought it would be, but spicy and hot. Just like the man who was feeding her. When he started taking her harder, his body pounding into hers, Beth let her body go and came four times before he threw back his head and howled. She held onto him when her own body seemed to shatter with him.

It was the most incredible, sexy thing she had ever seen, and she came twice more before he dropped over her and rolled to his back. Laying over him, she closed her eyes. Tomorrow, she thought, they'd talk tomorrow. Right now she wanted to rest up so that she could do this again. Christ, she hoped that she'd never get tired of this man. And didn't think it was even possible.

The room was pitch black when something woke her. Nate was moving to get up when the light flared on. It took her several seconds to realize that he was dressed and she was still in the bed. Beth asked him what was going on.

"Benton." She stood up. Her clothing was everywhere. She wasn't even sure she could wear any of it. When Nate put his hands to the side of her face, she looked at him, panicky. "Breathe. And think of wearing something warm and strong. Boots too."

Nodding, she looked down at her body and realized that she was wearing the first thing that she'd thought of. A warm coat that hung to her knees, a hat the covered her ears, and pants that were as soft as anything that she'd ever worn. Looking at Nate, she knew that what she had on would never do, and thought of what he had on. Leather pants, boots that were practical, not pretty, and a tee shirt that was long sleeved. He handed her a jacket that was too big when she put it over her arms, but it seemed to form to her as she zipped it up. And for reasons that she couldn't explain, even to herself, she wasn't freaked out about it. Smiling, she kissed him on the mouth, then they moved to the door.

Following him out of the room, she could hear the buzzer, a loud annoying sound, going off everywhere. Whatever Benton was up to, it had the household scrambling. As they all tumbled onto the lawn, she looked up when she noticed that they all were too.

The big monster from the other day was spraying more fire over them, and he was dipping down so close to where they were that she was sure that it was only a matter of time before he hit one of them. Beth looked around, wondering why no one was running for cover.

"He can't touch us. At least we hope he can't." Beth looked over at Kate when she spoke beside her. "If he lands, then we'll try and kill him. But until then, we let him wear himself out. I understand that you've spoken to him, so you know what I'm talking about."

"He's done this before, then." Kate told her that he was forever trying to kill them. Especially Remy. "Why? I mean, I know that he's pissed off about something, but what it is?"

"We won't die."

Before she could comment on that, not even sure what she'd say, Benton landed near where they were, but on the other side of the magical line that she'd never noticed until just now. As one the men moved toward him, either on foot or flying. Each of them were very careful not to get too close, but arrows were shot at the monster, as well as magic from some of the others. Beth moved to help, then she stopped to watch them.

They weren't a team. The couples worked together for the most part, but as a whole they seemed to just do a little damage here and there on the creature before moving on to someplace else on his body. Remy and Skylar had each other's back. The dragons flew in tandem, but never interacted with the others if they could help it. They didn't get in their way, but they didn't help either. Each of them were strong, did a good job when they engaged, but they weren't making any kind of progress that she could see.

Beth did not go to help, which even she could see was a lost cause. Not just for their group, but for the monster as well, it seemed. As she stood there, her sword in her hand, she thought of the dream that she'd had and kept an eye on the monster. When Remy came to stand in front of her, more than likely to ask her what the fuck she was doing, Beth pointed to Benton.

"He has no idea what to do with his body. It's like he's bought it because it was on sale, but there were no instructions for it." Remy turned as well, not saying a word as she continued to point out his mistakes. "He has great claws at his feet. But instead of using them to swipe at one of us, he is gripping the ground as if he is afraid of falling. Even though he can't go over the barrier, which I'm assuming we can, he doesn't use them to take one of the others out when they accidently fly over it. He protects his chest, like he's not sure if the scales there will keep his...heart, I suppose, safe. This team is no different. Each of them seem to be working to get him to die, but they're not very effective in the way that they're going about it. See?"

She wasn't sure what she should have expected from him. Anger for sure. Even him telling her that she was nothing but a woman and had only just joined them. That she knew nothing of warfare, which she didn't, and that she would be better served joining them in this fight rather than picking his men apart with her useless information. But he watched

Benton with her, pointing out other things that she'd seen, even a couple that she'd not.

"He favors his arm still. Even though it is no longer injured, it hung at his side for a long time, and he still treats it as if it is of no use to him. And as you pointed out, he protects his chest with his claws rather than using them to defeat us." Beth told him to look at his tail. "It only lays there, not even curling about him to protect his body. If I were him I'd be swinging it to and fro to try to take us out, knock someone to their bottoms and step upon their bodies. He does not use it for anything at all but to be at his hind end."

They both watched carefully now, pointing out things that not only Benton was doing, or not doing most of the time, but his men and women as well. They weren't a team, he said, he could see that now. Each of them had their own agenda, and they were sticking to it no matter the cost to their exhaustion. And that was what was going to get them killed, Beth thought. They were fighting a war against themselves rather than waging one single war against their enemy.

"What must we do to defeat him? I am surely sick of fighting this war with him only to come up short. I have plans to be with my lady and go to the shoreline that she's told me so much about. To make love there without the threat of monsters, any of them, coming for me." She looked at him then, thinking that he frightened her somewhat. He was a man like none other, and with a single swipe of his blade, he could end her. And Beth had only just discovered that she didn't want to die, not yet at any rate. "I can read your mind. And while I can understand that you'd think these things of me, I am hurt that you should."

"I'm sorry." He bowed before her and asked her again what they needed to do. "He can't cross the barrier, can he? I mean, he's pretty much stuck out there unless we go to him."

"Nay, he cannot come inside these walls. If you suggest that we leave him to his business and we go to ours, then I would have to ask that you have another plan. He is keeping me from my mine." He winked at her, and she had a feeling that his plans were more along the line of making love on those shorelines than just enjoying the water. "And you would be right."

"Okay. But just so you know, that's very rude of you. But we need to regroup. Pull back and talk about this. I've always been pretty good at seeing the whole, but my ideas of executing them are a little off. I don't know what you all can do, but I can see that you're as bad as him, not utilizing your gifts as best you can." He asked her what that might be. "Each other. You depend on one another to do the job, but there is no job that you're all working to get done other than killing Benton. And you will have to be a group, not several going for the same goal only at the risk of each other. Look at Skylar. You've left her. What is she doing?"

He watched her for several minutes. She was fighting her own war with Benton, as were the others, digging into different parts of him, hoping for something to happen. Remy turned to her.

"No one has stepped up to help her. I don't believe that they'd let her be harmed, but they've not done anything to ensure that she does not exhaust herself. And that is what we are about, exhausting our resources instead of pooling them together." Beth nodded. "You have seen our weaknesses. Where do we need to strike at Benton to take him down?"

"The part of him that he protects the most, and not one of you have even tried to get to, his chest. I mean, you go there, try and stab him, but when that doesn't work, you move on and try another tactic. Like fishing in a pond that you keep moving around in, hoping for better results with your pole." Remy watched Benton this time, and Beth could see that he understood. When he put his fingers to his mouth and whistled, every one of the brotherhood backed from Benton and came to where they were. If they worked like that when fighting, she thought they could have won by now. Benton laughed when they were all standing too far for him to reach even if he could have.

"You have given up so easily, Rembrandt? You have tired yourself so quickly? I cannot believe that the great and powerful Rembrandt the Warrior has given me this win. Whatever shall I do when we meet again? I know, I shall crush you beneath my power and make you submit to me. But it will be for naught; I will kill you." No one answered his taunts. And when he roared at them to come back and let him kill them, Remy looked at her.

"You have helped us. When we next meet him, we'll be better prepared." She nodded. "Has Nate told you of your death? The one that he sees in his dreams?"

"Benton kills me." He nodded. "But I'm not going to let that happen. He can try, but I'm not ready to give up. I have someone in my life that has made me happy. And I'm pretty sure that between the two of us, we can figure this out so we can all have a life, don't you think?"

"Aye, I can see that." Remy started to step away when he turned back to her. "Hector said that when you arrived, we'd be stronger. I thought it was that you were going to be the most powerful of us all. And you are, just not with muscle. Your thinking, it's what is going to get us out of this war and on to better things. For that, I am forever grateful for you coming to us. You will be our strongest weapon as yet."

Beth watched Benton as he stood there screaming at them to come back. When the last of them but her and Nate moved into the house and the door was closed, he roared out his frustrations and said he'd be returning. Neither of them spoke to the monster, but Beth had a feeling that he thought he'd already won. And that was going to be his biggest mistake.

Chapter 8

The mural on his back was gone. Now it was just markings, like the ones all over his body. When he tried to remember the last time he'd seen, or even felt it, he had no idea. Nate had been so focused on Beth and her family that he'd forgotten it. And now it was gone.

"What about the dreams? Are they still coming to you?" He nodded at Chris. "Damn, I'd hoped that they'd disappear as well. Does she still get killed?"

"Yes. Every time. It's the same, her body torn in half and tossed away like she is nothing. She is everything to me, Chris. I don't think I'd survive without her near me." Nate sat down and tried to think about what this might mean, the drawing on his back being gone. When Rick and Leo joined them, Chris brought them up to speed. But Rick was more focused on the stacks of papers and books that had been brought by the other man.

Chris and Kate were living in the real world, for lack of a better term. Chris had become a teacher, teaching sentence structure and Edgar Allen Poe to fifth graders. Kate had been working as a florist, putting together baskets of plants for people who had no idea what kind of monsters she'd seen and killed. And weekly now, they'd bring information, as well as anything they could lay their hands on to bring them up to speed for when this war was over. And it was when, not if. Nate had never been so anxious for something to end as he was this. He was sure the rest of them were as well.

"You've been gone for three days, so what sort of information do you have for us? And so you know, I get first dibs on the books. I'm slowly running out of things to read now that we're not fighting so much." Chris grinned at Rick. "So how is fifth grade going for you? You think you'll pass this time? I'm thinking you're a mite old to be there for so long."

"Fuck you." Chris pointed to a stack of boxes that Nate had helped him bring in from his car. "I got those for *everyone* to read. And so you know, not much has changed in the last year. We're still in a crisis everywhere with stupid stuff that we can't control. Prices are going up, and things are pretty much shit when you watch the news. Kate and I have stopped watching it in favor of looking for homes for the rest of you."

"You're having no trouble with the tats then?" Chris said it was just as they'd thought, no one could see them except others like them. Leo let out a long breath before continuing. "How many houses are there for us? I know that Remy and Skylar are going to build here if they don't do this other thing with Hector's world, but I want something that I can have a large yard in, plenty of trees, as well as a mountain."

As Rick and Leo talked over the file that Chris had brought back with him that was filled with housing specs and pictures, Nate thought of the conversation that he'd had with Lyle this morning. The man was at his wit's end when it came to his wife. And truthfully, so was he. The woman would not stop interfering in things that had nothing to do with her. And he was still pissed about his breakfast yesterday morning.

"I cooked for you." Nate had glanced at Ann, who was

playing with her grandson and seemed to be pissed herself. But Ruth told him to have a seat and she'd show him. "You are going to have to cut out the carbs and some of the fat you're eating. I know this will be difficult for you to get used to, after eating like you have been, and it'll be something of a trial for you. But you'll see. In a few days not only will you feel better, but you'll see that you didn't need all that food anyway."

He looked at the food on the plate she'd set in front of him. There was a single egg that didn't look right. Two slices of toast that had some kind of globs of yellow stuff on them. Bacon that looked like something made from a toy he'd played with as a child where dough went in, but this shape came out the other end. And he was pretty sure the dough would taste better than this shit did. A glass of orange juice that looked more like puss than made from actual oranges, as well as about half a cup of the smallest diced up potatoes he'd ever seen. He looked at her.

"I know what you're thinking. But you'd be wrong. Like you are about what you're eating. You're thinking that I'm helping you too quickly. But I assure you—"

"That's not at all what I was thinking. I'm pretty sure that you don't even want to know half of what is going on in my head at this moment. And even if you said you did, I'd not let go of the things that are circling in my head to say to you. Also, you're not helping me one bit, and you damn well know it. Like I said before, you see something you want to be done to your liking and fuck anyone else that gets in your way." He looked at Ann. "Can I have some real food please? And enough to fill me?"

Ruth pointed at him when she spoke next. "No. You're not going to make that poor woman make you something to eat when I've gone to a lot of trouble for you. Look, you just don't see the things that I do. That food, and the amount you were eating, is going to kill you. You don't want that. I know you're a reasonable man who will see, in a couple of days, that I was right. Now eat. You'll love how good it tastes. Better than all that fatty stuff you were eating before. I only have your best interests at heart, you have to see that." He stood up and she backed from him. "I don't care how big you are, Nathaniel, you're not thinking sensibly, that's all. I'm right in this. You eat your breakfast, and then you and I will go over what you're to have for lunch and dinner too."

He took the plate to the trash can and tossed it in, food and all. Then he went to the cabinets and got a large glass and poured juice, real freshly squeezed orange juice this time, to the rim. Draining that, he poured a second one before he sat down again. Ruth huffed at him.

"I don't think you're thinking this through. You know that I'm right, and you're just being stubborn. Now, stay right there and I'll whip you up something again. But I won't have you wasting food, Nathaniel." She reached for the skillet on the stove and he took it from her. "You know that I'm right. I'm always right, and you just have to let me show you."

"I'm a shifter that has been enhanced. If I don't eat my required five thousand calories or more a day, I might have to find other things to eat. And then that will make me cranky. Trust me, Ruth, I'm a hell of a lot nastier when I'm hungry." He stood near her then, letting a little of his bear go as he loomed over her. "Do you know what a bear will do to his food before he finishes it off? He plays with it until it's so broken that it doesn't fight him when he finally tears into it. Eating it raw and leaving parts of his food all over the place. You would more than likely be stringy and bitter, but if you try to pull this shit on me again, I will test that."

126

"You're a mean person, and I hope that my daughter breaks your heart. If you even have one." Nate sat down just as Ann handed him some food. It was a dozen fried eggs over two diced up potatoes. When Ruth reached for it, he grabbed her wrist and held it. "You're hurting me. I'm only trying to help you. Why must you be so mean to me all the time? Why am I the only one that seems to care about people, even though they don't appreciate it? I'm only trying to help."

Nate took her to the floor, her sobs getting louder as he twisted her wrist to get her there. When Lyle came in, followed shortly by Beth, neither of them said a word, but sat at the table with him. When he let Ruth go, he watched her. There was something seriously wrong with this woman. She stood up, glaring at him as she held her bruising wrist to her body.

"What did I ever do to you? You know that I'm right. I don't understand why you won't just do it my way. You're as bad as Lyle. He never listens to me either. And all I want to do is help." Her crying became a gasping like sob, and the tears, seemingly ever present on this nutball's face, ran down her face like a river after a great rain. "I'm not going to stop. You're going to have to do as I want so that you'll be healthy. That's all I want, for you to listen to me, and you won't. No one listens to me here."

Nate said nothing as he ate his breakfast. He needed this much food to survive. And if she couldn't see it, then he was going to have a talk with Remy about getting her removed from the house and perhaps set up in one of the other houses that were going up all over the place. And it wasn't just his food either; he'd heard from others that she was pushing her ideas onto them as well. He'd had to spend over an hour with a woman named Lily just yesterday, trying to calm her.

"She said that I was raising my children wrong. Told me

127

that I was a bad momma. I'm not a bad momma, am I Nate?" He had told her she was not. "I gotta work, and since my husband was killed being one of them monsters, I gotta take them to daycare. And they get good care."

"They do. And I know for a fact that your children are well behaved and taken care of very well by you." She had nodded, still crying. "Lily, that woman is wrong. I hope you know that."

"She told me she was gonna tell the police about me leaving them all day with the daycare while I was out. I gotta work, Nate. I gotta be able to feed them." When she cried again, he held her in his arms. "That woman, she ain't coming in my house no more. I'll have to lock her out. She done went and told Mary that she needed to get out more and walk. The woman is ninety-four years old and can barely remember her name. How she gonna walk about, I ask you?"

"I know you take Mary for walks every day. And she loves when you bring the children over. You just keep doing what you are, and I'll have Remy talk to her." He picked up one of the children when they came to comfort their momma. "You keep an eye on her for me, will you, James?"

"Yes, sir. I'm gonna get a water pistol and use it on that old biddy. Momma said that is the best way to make a mean old cat scat." Nate had laughed and told the little boy that was a good idea. "You tell her that I'm gonna shoot her, Mr. Nate. That'll keep her away."

"My lord?" He looked at Whey when he said his name, bringing him from his thoughts. The little guy had been hanging around with him for the last couple of days, answering questions about this and that. "The lady of the waters would like to have a word with you and the others. There is...she has done something, and now she fears that she should have

128

spoken to Lord Remy about it first."

"Does it have to do with Benton?" He said that sadly, it did. "All right. I'll have Remy and the others come in here. Is that all right with you?"

"Thank you, my lord. She feels badly for her actions, but in my opinion, humble as it is, I think she did the right thing." Nate nodded and looked around the room that had gone quiet. "You go on, sir. I've a handle on things here."

Nate wasn't sure what that meant, but he reached for Remy and he said that they would all meet him in the dining room. As he finished up his meal, a second then third plate of food brought to him, Nate talked to Lyle and Beth as if Ruth wasn't just in the other room still wailing. When her sobbing and demands to have his food taken away and fixed properly got louder, even Ann began to ignore her.

Remy came into the room and looked at Ruth, who had come to join them, no doubt not getting the attention that she wanted in the kitchen. She was still nursing her wrist and glaring at Nate. With a small shake of his head, Remy smiled back. The man was going to get an earful from Ruth, he'd bet. And at the moment, Nate didn't care. They all looked at Whey when he cleared his throat for attention.

"The lady of the water, my lord. She had stopped the flow to the lake that the monster bathes in. And she fears that perhaps she has angered him, and he'll take this out on the company here." Remy asked him what he meant by bathing in. "He lies in it. Well he was…now he can only sit in it. But soon that won't be happening, as the water is drying up. The water is rich in magic. It's what we have used for centuries to water the special plants that we grow. Seasonal ones for certain times of the year. Then there are the beauties that seldom come. It's a sight to behold, my lords, so beautiful that you'd—"

Pitch told him to get on with it, but Remy stopped him. "You mean that's what enhanced him so that he's whole again? A bath in this water? It's that powerful?" Pitch shrugged when Whey did, and said that had never happened before. "But it has now. He got in the water and now he's strong again."

"Maybe it's a combination of the drugs he took and the water." Everyone turned to Ann as she brought in cinnamon rolls and tea. "You said yourself that he was bigger. Perhaps that magic from the other world gave him something extra that the water just happened to be able to mix with. You be knowing as well as I, my lord, that things are never just a simple case of just being. You want some more rolls? I have them in the oven now should you." When she left, all Nate could think of was that this place was bedlam. Pure and simple.

"You mean something like an additive to this other drug?" Lyle started pacing the room. "That could work. If I had a bit of the mixture and some of the water, I could tell you for certain. I could...well, I'd need a lab and some equipment, but if I could—"

"Lyle, I'll not have you going to some lab working on things you know nothing about. You're going to make things worse, like you always do. Just take your medicine I laid out for you and go on back to our room and take a nap. You've been up for a while now." Ruth stood up and put out her hand to Lyle to no doubt do as she was telling him. "Come on now, Lyle, you've bothered these people long enough with your fanciful tales." And of course she was ignored.

"I have it in me as well, the drug I mean. And I'm sure that Pitch could persuade the lady to give you a bit of the water to test as well." Nate felt embarrassed when no one said anything. "Or not. It was just an idea."

"No, no, that's wonderful. How about the water, young Pitch? Do you think you can get me a bit? I'd need at least a cup or more if she can let me test it." Whey said that he'd get it and took off. "Now. What can I use for a lab?"

Remy patted him on the back. "We'll have everything you need as soon as you think of it. And while you're at this, I'd like to introduce you to some other magic that is here. You might fit in very well."

As they walked away, Nate looked at Beth. She was watching her dad move along with Remy like she envied him. He pulled her into his arms and kissed her on the mouth quickly. The rest of them laughed as they went back to work. Ruth glared at him once again and left as well.

"You can go and help him. I don't know why, but I never thought of what sort of engineering you and your dad did." She smiled at him. "You're very sexy when you look at me like that."

"That's not saying much. Just a bit ago you claimed I was the most beautiful woman you'd ever seen, when all I was doing was playing with the dogs in the yard. You have a screwed up way of telling ordinary from pretty." He kissed her again. "But I would like to go and see your lab. I bet it's as state of the art as the rest of this place."

"You have no idea. And the more you think you need, the more you can have. Much like our room." He paused a moment before he said what he really wanted to. "Your mother. We're going to have to do something about her, and soon. She's started to get on everyone's nerves the way she moves in and tries to take over their lives."

"I'd say I'll talk to her, but it won't do any good. Mom thinks she's the only one that knows better and we should all just do it like she wants. I guess I never realized what a pain in the ass she was until I moved out. Poor Dad. No wonder he calls me all the time. I must be the only person he can talk to that doesn't tell him he's doing something wrong."

"You're right about that. I've never seen a more depressing, stubborn woman in all my life." Beth sat down and he joined her. "I wanted to thank you for helping us train. The input that you've given us, I think it's going to help a great deal."

"You guys would have figured it out eventually. I guess you could say I was just a new set of eyes." Where her mom was a pushy know-it-all, Beth was just the opposite. Her new eyes, as she called them, had made them work together, and that was what they needed. From the beginning, that was what she'd told them.

They were going to win this. He knew it. Now all he had to do was make sure that she didn't get killed. The dreams were getting more violent. They were waking him up at night, and the only way he could go back to sleep was to make love to Beth. Not that that wasn't a wonderful thing, but she was sleeping fitfully too, and there had to be an end soon. Just not with her death.

When she left him to go to the labs that he was sure were filled with every gadget known to man, he went to find Ruth. He was going to try his best to make her understand that she had to back off and leave everyone alone. He, like Beth, doubted that it would work, but he would try. She was his future mother-in-law, and he didn't want to have to murder her to get along.

~~~

Master wasn't happy. They were forever not playing fairly and letting him simply kill them. They had just left him there when he was winning. In another few minutes, he would have had them just where he wanted. Rembrandt had called them group away just as he was ready to finish them once and for all.

"Are you sure about that? It looked to me like you were standing there letting them pound on you. Have you gone to the lake to get your wounds taken care of? That woman with the white fingers, she sure did burn you a little." Mary again. Would she ever leave him in peace? "Nay, I will not. You have me here, and when you need someone to tell you like it is, then I'm going to be the one you call on. And you didn't answer my question. Did you think to go to the lake to heal, or have you had your bottom handed to you and went home to sulk in your cave?"

"I do not call upon you. You just come here in my head. And I was tired. You've not any idea how hard it is on me to fight with so many at one time. I came here so that I'd not drown in my waters whilst I healed. So there." He moved to the opening of the cave and looked down at the lake. "In a few more days, less perhaps, I will no longer fit in the water, I think. As it is now, I must take great handfuls and pour it over me. That is not fair of him either. Rembrandt has much to answer for, I think."

"You should have told him to stop it while you were there with him. He's not a reasonable man on most things, but in this, having you die isn't going to solve anything. Yes, you should have told him that he must return the waters to where they were." He should have. But he'd been busy keeping himself from being hurt too badly. "When do you go back to finish this, Benton? Soon? I should hope today. They need to be taught a lesson. And even though you are all we have left to do so, you can win this now, I think."

"Why today?" She didn't answer him, and he moved to

the waters and sat in them. "'Tis not even deep enough for me to sit in now. Yes, he has much to answer for."

"He does." Ward now. They switched around too much for him to keep up sometimes. "You must go back today. You have played around enough, and we would like for you to end this. Things have been going on far too long, and Rembrandt has gotten a big head. I want you to go there and murder him and all those people."

"I am in charge. I say when I go and when I kill him." He didn't sound very convinced of that, even to himself. "I was going in the morning. It matters little if I attack in the night or day, so I might as well rest well and go during the day when I can see better. They'll have that protection up all the time now. I should have killed him long ago. But in the daylight, I'll be able to finish this. It's gone on far too long." He waited for one of them to tell him they'd said that. When they didn't mention it, he filled his hand with water and poured it over his tattered wing.

"I believe that is good thinking, going in the daylight." Dolin this time. When this was done, Master was going to order them to leave him so he could have a peaceful life. Without them. He poured water over the wound at his arm now and watched as it not only healed, but looked as if he'd never been touched by magic there. "You will need to save what water you have. When you go there tomorrow you will be wounded again, and perhaps the water might not be there when you return. Should that happen, you'll look nasty to your subjects."

"I think you might be right on that. I shall... I don't have any buckets to hold it in. What should I use?" Ward said that he didn't know, but Remy might have something. "Yes, but I don't want him to know that I've found this place. He is a good friend, but I think he'd take my magic from me."

"He is not your friend, dumbass. Rembrandt is your enemy. How many times must you be told that?" He hated Mary in that moment. "I don't like you very much either. You are the most forgetful man I have never known. If you were to go to him now, do you suppose that he'd invite you in for tea? Or perhaps a barbeque? Don't be so dense all the time. He is not your friend. He'd kill you if he was given the chance, and you know this."

"I have had a great deal on my mind of late, so I cannot be made to remember every little detail as you seem to. Trying to kill Rembrandt and his brotherhood is one of many things I'm working on. Do you have any idea how taxing that is on my head?" She said that he didn't have much to work with, so it mattered little. "You must leave me in peace. I should like to never hear from you again."

When she huffed at him, he thought she would continue to speak. Just last week he'd told her she talked too much and wished her gone, and for hours on end she sang. He was sure she was making up the words to the idiotic song, but no matter how much he ordered, or even begged, her to stop, she didn't for nearly half a day.

Once this was finished, he'd get rid of her once and for all. Tomorrow he would go and kill the brotherhood and Rembrandt, and rule. He was far superior to any of them, he'd just been...well, he'd been playing with them, he decided. He was bigger as well, and he knew what he was about. Instead of asking them to come to him, thinking that they should think it an honor, he was going to just get them where he wanted, then kill them. It was well past time for him to be in charge.

He laid in the water for as long as he could. When he felt as if he'd gotten all that he could from it, he went to his lair again. The plan had been perfect. What he'd not counted on was the magic being up all the time now. But he knew now and would only have to adjust things a little to overcome it. Since he'd had time to think, he supposed he should have known that someone would think to put the barrier up all the time. The stupid woman and man that he'd spoken to, that had been a small mistake, but easily taken care of. But as it was, he made a small adjustment to his plans and laid down. Tomorrow was going to be a great day.

The noise outside his realm woke him with a rush. His chest hurt where his heart might have been, and he had to tell himself that he was bigger than anything that dared to come out of the woods. As he made his way to the opening of his cave, he saw nothing around and nearly went back to his bed when he heard it again. He came out of his dwelling and blew fire over the remaining trees to light the way. There stood Rembrandt.

"What is the meaning of this? Go back to your compound, Rembrandt. I'm to kill you in the morning. It's entirely too dark for me to see you properly, and I've not had enough rest. Go now, and I'll kill you soon." Rembrandt laughed at him. That was when he saw the others. "What is this about? You have no right to come here. And where is my waterway? What have you done to it? No matter. Just let it come back to me so that I may heal when you cause me harm. And buckets. I should like for you to give me some buckets so that I might steal some of the water away and have it in my home. Go now and do as I have said."

"I don't think so. We've talked to the lady of the lake, and she had decided that rather than you having her magic, she would rather see the water gone. So little by little she has been diverting the water to other lakes. At least until we've killed you. I assured her it wouldn't be long now." Master came out of his lair and moved toward the man. "You've been benefiting from it a great deal, Benton, but now it's time for you to stop."

"I will say when I shall stop. I have told you countless times, I am Master. You will bend to my will, Rembrandt. I tire of these games with you. Yes, I have been better since using the water, and you'll tell her to not keep me from it. Go now. And in the morning, after I've had a proper rest, I'll come and kill you." He looked down at the others as they stood there waiting. "You all will need to die. And it would help me greatly if you were to let me kill you quickly. I have a plan that you're making me get behind on. Should you like, I can kill a few of you now, but on the morrow, it will be Rembrandt's turn."

"We thought we'd interrupt your rest now. Like you did ours the other night." Master said nothing, but did swipe his claw out and knock several trees down in their direction. No one was close enough for him to harm, but he did feel better for making them look. Until Remy laughed harder. "You're a big clumsy nothing, aren't you, Benton? You can only kill because of your size. Have you ever purposely killed someone that wasn't Ward or Dolin?"

"I shall kill you. And your wife, I did murder her while you were out doing deeds for others. You forget that part, do you not? She was a tasty morsel, your wife. I had her for dinner. And those children of yours as well." Rembrandt said nothing, he didn't even look to be upset. Master wanted to stomp his foot, but Ward warned him that it was childish and might make Rembrandt laugh yet again. "Have you thought of her screams for mercy, Rembrandt? I have heard them when I need something to cheer me up."

"Do you? And how is that, when you never had anything to do with her or my children's deaths except to hire someone to kill them? You know as well as I, and I think I have pointed this out to you before, you hid behind the trees as others took her life. But my children, they died bravely as well. I doubt that they made a peep as they hid from the men that were there that day. I doubt that you'll go as quietly. Nor will you be as brave as them. I think you to scream like a small child, begging for mercy that you have shown no one since you were sent here. You will die a very horrific and painful death, Benton. Mark my words on that." He looked at them again; they were tight together, as if they were awaiting the signal to attack him again. "What you see before you now is my family. Not to replace the ones that I lost long ago, but ones that have come to help, to stand beside me, and to be there when I need them. You could have had such a family, Benton. Not now, but you could have at one time. Someone to love and —"

"Will you stop calling me by that horrid name? I am Master. Lord to all that you see and more. I will rule you, Rembrandt. And when you are dead, I will fuck your wife and family." He set flames to them and watched in horror as nothing more than the trees around them burned. "What magic is this? I demand that you give it to me as well. Rembrandt, you have never played well. I have asked you countless times to let me kill you, and here you stand, tormenting me endlessly. Die so that I may rule now."

"You will never rule. And you cannot rule me if you should kill me. I think you have something wrong with your head if you think that. As for my wife? You should know that she will hurt you, much like she has before, and not be bothered in the least bit about you trying to fuck her. We all know that you have nothing between your legs."

He roared at them, and that was when the woman with the white fingers attacked. She burned into him; his scales melted, the power of it was so hot. As he tried to get away from her, he saw the dragons coming for his eyes. There was nothing he could do to stop it when one of them stabbed him there. Master fell back on the earth just as something tore into his wings. He had to get away or he would die.

Moving as quickly as he could, he brushed them away from him. Or he tried. Rembrandt hit him with his own sword, the magic of it burning deeply into his flesh. Even before he could get to his lair, he knew his left wing was gone, and his arm, mended before, was now broken again. The water would have to work hard when they left, or he'd not be fit to fight on the morrow. He was nearly to the back of the lair when he heard nothing. Not a sound at all.

As suddenly as they attacked, harmed him for no reason, they were gone. He looked back to where they had been aiming their magic at him…the place was muddy with their tracks and his blood. But they were nowhere to be seen, their swords and magic gone with them. Crawling back to the water to pour it over his fresh wounds, Master was in the woods again when he realized that he'd passed over the bed of magical water that was the only thing that would save him now. Going back and forth several times, he realized that the bed, the cradle that held his water, was no longer. The lake bed that he'd only just sat upon not an hour ago was as dry as the earth in his cave.

"Rembrandt, I'm going to enjoy killing you," Master screamed in the dark night, nearly crying for the unfairness of it all. Rembrandt had come here, harmed him, then left him without means to repair himself. The man was forever trying to kill him. "And for what reason? I have done nothing to make him do this to me. Nothing." And he'd not said when he would be bringing him the buckets, not that they'd do him any good now.

Well, tomorrow he would pay. And when he was the victor, Master was going to show him what a master he was. Rembrandt would die.

Chapter 9

Beth watched the faeries. They were amazingly fast, and they seemed to know just what to do with only a single movement from Ryiah. They were like birds, moving as a single unit no matter where they were led. Beth thought she could watch them for hours, their color alone enough to make her wish she was up there with them. When her dad sat next to her, she smiled at him

"Your mother wants to go home now. I think she's upset with everyone because they won't take her *advice*. Not that it's ever that. More like she plows her way into something and expects you to simply go along. I guess I did for a very long time." She asked him what he wanted to do. "Stay. And if it's okay with you and the rest of the group here, I'd like to. Very much so."

"I'd like that too, Dad. I've forgotten how much fun you are when we do things together. Mom, she's not going to be happy with you. But Remy said that you came up with a serum to help weaken Benton, and he's thrilled to death with something going his way for a change. He also said that you were going to help them with a great many other things as well." Her dad only nodded. "Dad, I'm in love with Nate. I know that it's really fast and all, but I really do love him."

"I can tell that you do, sweetheart. And I have to tell

you, I'm a little in love with him too." He laughed. "Every time he stands up to your mother? I just want to go and hug him. I think he's the reason that I feel so good lately. And since I've noticed how easy it is—well, not easy, but better for everyone—I've been telling her to fuck off a lot more too. He's been doing what I should have been doing all along."

"She's a force, Mom is." He nodded. "We're going to war when that monster returns. They're going to try and kill him. Thanks to you, they have a good chance. Then things will get back to normal around here. I'm not sure what that means for Nate and me, but I'm going to stay here."

"I understand they've been going at this for a long time. I guess we were lucky that they centralized here instead of trying to take over the world right away. It had something to do with some stones and Remy. I guess this Benton person has been fixated on Remy for a very long time." She'd heard that as well. "Beth, I'm going to file for divorce as soon as I can find myself an attorney. Your mother can have the house, the car. All I want is to be with you. The rest...it meant more to her than it ever did me anyway. I just can't take it anymore, and I've decided that I don't have to. I want to be able to show my face in places. Go where I want dressed the way I want to be. Have some fun. I never realized...well, that's not true. I knew what sort of person your mother was, but it was easier just to let her have her way than to be beaten up by her. Not physically, but she worked a number on me mentally. I won't have it any more."

"Good. I'm so glad for you, Dad. I think the reason that I moved out so soon after high school was that I was embarrassed by her. And hurt. She had a way of cutting me to the quick all the time. I got to the point where I'd not bring people home anymore. Not even dates. It was just too hard to explain to people that she wasn't being mean, just a know-it-all. But I came to realize that she really is a mean person. And she tries to cover it up by telling people she was only being helpful." Beth could tell that her dad was hurt. She was as well. "I'm so sorry, Dad. I know that you love her very much."

"No, no, that's not it. I ache because she hurt you so much. But as for loving her? I used to. I think for these last few years I just got used to her being there and thought that I still loved her. And in a small way, I still do. But I need to be my own man again. Not this shell of a person that she turned me into." He laughed bitterly. "I'm an intelligent man who holds a doctorate in three different fields of engineering; I can dress myself, eat when I'm hungry, and drive a car. Yet I found myself letting my wife take that all away from me all the time. And for no other reason than I was too overwhelmed to deal with her."

When one of the little faeries came to them, Beth sat very still. Honestly, she was terrified of hurting one of them, but when he landed on her father's outstretched leg, she kept an eye on them both. After a minute, the little blue man moved up his leg and then sat near his hand. The two of them regarded each other carefully before the little man spoke.

"My name is Woolly. Really it's Woodsworth, but that's what they've been calling me for a long while now." Her dad told him his name. "Lyle. I like that name. Strong one, it is. I was wondering if you could give me a hand."

"If I can. I'm not sure what I can do for you. I'm not magical like the rest of you are." Woolly looked at her, then at her dad as he continued. "May I see your wings again? I know that it's terribly rude of me, but I find them to be fascinating, if you want to know the truth."

"Course. Don't touch 'em though. They're very sexual."

143

Her dad snatched his fingers back so quickly that he nearly knocked Woolly, who was laughing, off his lap. "I was joshing you there, feller. I don't get to do that often and have someone react. You're a good, funny man. Go on ahead, have you a look see. While you're about that, I'll tell you what I need."

Her dad held out his hand and Woolly jumped into it. When he spread out his wings, Beth laughed when her father curled his other hand into a tight fist. He wasn't taking any chances, apparently.

"As I was saying, I'm in need of your help. You see, I'm in charge of the sheep in the pastures. Not many of them left nowadays, but we try. Problem I'm having is that there isn't enough grass growing where they are. I'm thinking that we need something to hype up the feeding area. Nothing that will hurt them, mind you. Can't have that. But something that can get the grass growing a little stronger than it has been." Dad asked about manure. "Don't have much of that either. Cow is the best, horse too. But we don't have any of them around. You done with my wings?"

"Yes, I'm sorry. They're very beautiful." Woolly thanked him. "How would one go about getting cows? I mean, that would be the best solution. Perhaps you know of a farm that would sell you some of their offerings?"

"There's a pasture not far from where I tend the sheep, but for me to go there…well, I'm sure you can see that someone might not take me too serious should I go and ask for his cow droppings. Could be you could talk it over with him." Woolly sat down on Dad's hand. "'Course, I don't know that he's around anymore either. Might have been taken by them other creatures. Mayhap we can have someone look into that. We don't steal, you know that, don't you? Against nature to take what don't be offered or given freely."

144

When the two of them left her, Beth thought by the end of the day her dad would either have a farmer helping them or he'd be the farmer. She had a feeling that her dad would make a great cattle rancher.

"May I join you?" She looked up and saw Ryiah standing over her. This woman, even more than Skylar, made her a little nervous. "I won't hurt you."

"I know that. I'm just a little shy around all this magic, I guess. Yes, please have a seat." When they were both on the lawn, two of the dogs came running up to them. "They're so friendly. I mean, I guess they would be with all the people around, but they also mind well."

"They've never peed in the house or anything else either. I think that when they were given to us, they were already trained not to do anything that would upset the household. They're the biggest stress relievers I've ever seen." Ryiah petted the dog on her lap as she continued. "We're ready, I think. Don't you? To take on Benton, I mean."

"I do. I know that I'm sort of the new person, but I think you'll stand a better chance with everyone working together like you are. Once he's hit the first time, I think he'll either back off or die after the second wave of attack." Ryiah said that her men were glad to be of service. "I was watching them a bit ago. They're so beautiful, but I'm guessing they can be just as deadly too. By the way, my dad is going to work with Woolly. Do you know him?"

"Somewhat. I try to remember all their names, but there are just too many of them. He asked me if he could talk to him. I don't know why they think I'm going to tell them no, but they do." The dogs took off when several children came out of the compound. They were giving them treats even as they tumbled all over them. "I've asked Remy to make sure that all the other people here are in the lower levels of the building. None of them will need to be out when he arrives, and I think we'll feel better not having to worry about them. The children will fare better too with their mothers about."

"Good idea. I know that there are a few houses here. And more are being built daily. I'm guessing that the apartment buildings are off site, and they'll know to take cover as well should he head in that direction?" Ryiah said she made sure that everyone was aware. "Okay, good. But why are you here now? I have a feeling that you're working up to something important."

"Your mom." Beth asked what she'd done now. "She said that she'll not be crowded into a room with children and adults she doesn't know. I told her she'd be safe there, and she said that she's been taking care of herself for years, that she's not going to huddle away when someone might need her. Nothing has reassured her that we don't need her help. I'm not sure what to do. I can't make her stay where she'll be safe, but I also can't have someone watching over her while this is going down. She'd get them both killed if I do that."

"She's the most stubborn person I've ever met, and she's going to get herself killed. I'm tempted to tell her to be on the field with us…maybe she can get Benton to do as we want. He is forever telling us we should just die. Maybe my mom can get him to do that for us instead." Beth looked around at the men and women working hard to save their lives. "I'm sorry, Ryiah. I'm sure that talking to her wasn't pleasant. I'll see what I can do about it. I'm not sure I can do anything, but I'll talk to her."

"Nah, I got her number. She and I have come to a sort of understanding. She sure does cry a lot, doesn't she? Anyway, I told her what would happen if she didn't stay hidden away, and she told me she was going to be just fine. I think she might be." Beth laughed when she did. "Your father, he's a good man. I like him very much. I think, if he'll stay on, he can do a lot for us when we start to make things come together. We have a long way to go, and we're going to need the help of men and women like him."

"He wants to stay. And he's divorcing my mom." Ryiah asked her how she felt about that. "Relieved first and foremost. Happy for him. I know that this has been a long time in coming. But also sad that he's at the point where he feels this is all he can do. And honestly, I think he's right. She's never going to change, and I'm glad that he can be his own man again. My dad is a wonderful person without her around."

Ryiah asked her if she'd like to get in some sword time and Beth said she would. The two of them were practicing when the ground beneath them started to rumble. It was the warning…Ryiah told her that Benton was on his way.

The yard emptied of people. Even the faeries seemed to know that they had to move as well. When everyone but the twelve of them were gone, Beth looked for Nate. He was coming toward her as his great bear, the biggest animal that he could use, and more than likely the strongest. Beth put her sword at her side as they waited. As much as it fit the situation, she hated using the swords. But Remy didn't have such trouble and spoke in a loud confident voice.

"It's showtime, my friends. May our swords fly true, the blood we spill not be our own, and may all of us come out victors on the other side in all of this." They spread their wings wide just as Benton came through the trees. Beth had only just realized today that they were there, and was glad for the extra magic that came with them.

~~~

147

Master thought that he'd been quiet, but there they stood, all in a line, as if waiting for him to kill them. Rembrandt took several steps forward, his body nearly naked and in battle mode. His body was so marked up with tattoos that Master wondered if he might get some himself. Master had seen him thusly a great many times before all of this had begun. Rembrandt told him once that he fought better when he had nothing in his way. Master thought him showing off. That was what it had to be.

"You have decided to let me kill you, Rembrandt? It is about time that you have seen me for what I am. Ruler and master. Come closer so that I might remove your head. Be assured that once you are dead, the others will follow closely behind so that you can watch over me while I make this world my own." Rembrandt only stood there with the large blade on his shoulder. "You have a request before I kill you? All right then. But I will tell you, I'm not going to have mercy on any of the people that have been trying to harm me. I am finished with the lot of you."

"We're not here to surrender, Benton. We're going to kill you. Today. And when you are gone, we're going to celebrate greatly. Why, I think we'll have drink and merriment for several days after you have become one with the earth. Sad to ruin such a lovely place, but there you have it. You'll be dead and we'll be better off." Rembrandt looked behind him, then at him again. "Have you any last words, Augustus Benton Hill?"

He knew that anger made him make mistakes. Ward and Dolin had told him again and again to keep his temper behind his teeth, to not let his anger rule his actions. But he was so mad at that moment that he flew at the man. When he touched not one part of him but was thrown back, he fell upon broken trees and one of them stabbed him through his belly. This was not going to help him, he thought.

Standing, he pulled the tree from his person and threw it at his enemy. It was then that he realized there was no barrier. When the branches sprayed over the yard behind them, Master knew that someone was helping him. Attacking again, he was nearly upon them when he was hit again, and this time he saw what it was.

The little bugs were everywhere, and they were pulling at the scales upon his chest and throat. He swatted at them the best he could, even holding some of his protection against his form, but they were too many and fast for him to do much.

Master had been unable to repair his one eye—the water had been taken from him to do so—but he could see what they were doing to hurt him. Why, his mind screamed at him, why was everyone against him being Master? Fighting them off seemed to make them angry, and they attacked him over and over. Then, suddenly, they were gone, and he was left with a large part of himself exposed, his scales laying at his feet. But that wasn't all that they'd done to him. They had used their little swords to cut him open too.

He was torn open in a great many places. His body hurt in areas that he'd never imagined pain to be centered. His feet were full of small splinters, and he pulled several out when he realized they were small arrows. They hurt, burned him, because of the magic he knew had been put upon them. Standing up again, he held his hand over his belly, where he bled badly, and started forward. Moving toward them again, Master saw the women huddled together and decided to take them out first. This time he knew that killing Rembrandt's woman would bring him to his knees so that he'd be able to kill him.

As they turned, he saw what they were about. The white fingered woman was lifting her arms. She was pointing her magic at him and he tried to back away, but he was too big, clumsy, and he tripped up. The magic from the woman burned into his arm and wing and they fell from him. He'd been cauterized, he realized. She had burned him so hotly that he'd not bleed, but he had lost his ability to fly, even if he'd been able to. For yesterday they'd injured him badly enough that he wasn't able to get more than a few inches off the ground before he fell to the earth again.

"Stop this right now. You cannot do this to me. I am Master."

They laughed; the women actually laughed at him and he felt his anger double. The darkness that took him was there, surrounding him in a way that made him sick with it. But he held on. If he let his rage go now, before he was ready, Rembrandt would hide and he'd not kill him. And killing Rembrandt was what was going to make him master of all.

Heat touched his chest, his other arm, and his belly. Every time he thought to move from the heat of their magic, he would feel them burning into him again. They were working as one, the women; their magic together was too strong for him, and they would not stop, no matter how many times he told them to. The women were fighting unfairly...they were winning, and he wasn't going to allow that. Reaching out for one of them, his hand filled and he pulled it to his mouth to smell. It wasn't Rembrandt, nor the woman that had hurt him so badly before. So tearing the offending human apart, he reached out again only to come up empty handed.

His hand was burned, and fingers that had grown back fell from his hand two, then three at a time. Even his claws, after sharpening them all night, were useless as they lay spent on the ground. Almost as soon as he realized that he was going to need to leave, to come back when he was stronger, the men joined the women and cut into his body with their magic and swords. Rembrandt too was hurting him. This was no way to treat a friend, he screamed, and still he hurt him.

The dragons, two at times and one larger at others, burned into his flesh. Their hot breath hit his chest where his scales were gone, and his neck hurt from the fire of them. Trying to use his own flame against them, all he did was get a mouth full of a vile liquid when he opened it to get in air. The dragons were dropping something terrible on him from buckets as they flew over him.

As it burned down his throat and to his belly, making him sicker as it went, he felt his chest armor fall away, his wing at his back being torn from him. Whatever they had poured on him took away all that the water had given him, and then some. Master was falling apart, and there was little to nothing he could do about it. Falling back again, Master tried to crawl away, get to the safety of his lair, when he heard Rembrandt.

"You're done? Already? You run and hide again, Benton? And here we were just beginning to have some fun." He roared out and told him he was not. That they were not doing as he wished. "And what would that be? To die, as you have said to us over and over? I'm sorry to disappoint you, Benton, but we're not going to do that. It is you that is going to die here this day, and I want you to know that you will never be mentioned again. Your name will not be spoken, even to get children to bed. You are finished."

Rembrandt flew to him then. Master was so broken, his arms so useless, that he could not even reach out to knock him away. But he lay there as his worst enemy landed upon him and walked to where his chest held his blackened heart.

Surely, Master thought, Rembrandt was going to fill it with magic, give him the ability to win this today.

The blade entered his chest, just enough to break through his ribs but not kill him. The cavern that had once been his heart felt hot, too hot for it to be helpful. He tried to look down at it, but he realized that his body no longer worked, that it was dead to him. This wasn't fair, and he was sure that Rembrandt had planned it that way. As he looked up at Rembrandt, he felt blood fill his eye, and he couldn't lift his arm to wipe it away.

"Rembrandt, please, you must help me. I am in great pain." The man stood there, his body hard with anger, covered in blood. Master realized it was his own blood, not that of his enemy as he had so hoped. "You and I, we were friends once. Please, do not let me die this way. I should like for us to be together in the afterlife. Come, let me kill you so that we can talk again when we are in the heavens."

The sword that his enemy held in his hands, no longer embedded in Master's chest, was not the one that Rembrandt had used on the battlefield. This one was bright with magic, bejeweled in a way that made him think it was meant for a king. A great man, someone like him. It was then that Master realized Rembrandt's intent...he was going to knight him. Smiling at his dear friend, he watched him as he walked to where his throat touched his shoulders. As Rembrandt swung the sword around, the brightness of it, every jewel, nearly blinded him.

"You wish to crown me too?" Rembrandt only shook his head. "That is a fine gift you give me, my friend. I will remember you fondly when I use it to kill you. Give it to me, please. Since you have given me a wonderful thing, I have decided to make your death quick. And that blade will be sharp enough to cut through your bones nicely. I thank you for it, my dear friend."

"He means to kill you, you fool." He told Mary he'd do no such thing. Rembrandt was his friend. But as he got closer to him, the blade arching higher and higher, Master had a feeling that she might be right. "I am forever right. And now you're to die because you were too stupid to heed my advice and stay on the other plane where you'd be safe."

The blade only touched his neck, he thought. There was no pain, not at first. But the longer it laid upon his flesh, he knew that Mary had indeed been correct. Rembrandt was going to murder him. And he didn't know why.

"Run," Ward and Dolin screamed at him. But there was no hope of him doing that. He could not move his body. He was broken until he got to the water. "He means to kill you. You must kill him. Hurry, before it is too late. You must fight back, Benton, or all will be lost. We'll not rule if you do not kill him now."

"I cannot."

As his neck started to burn hotter, he knew the moment that his head was no longer a part of him. Rembrandt had done it. He had murdered him. As his head started to scramble around for thoughts, for that was what it felt like it was doing, he watched his friend and realized in that moment that Rembrandt was a good man. But for him, it was too late.

Chapter 10

Nate held Beth in his arms as she sobbed. Had he not been close to her when it happened, he was not sure what he might have done. Holding her while the rest stood near the body of Benton, all he could think about was how were they going to tell Lyle.

"She just wouldn't listen to anyone. Mom thought that she knew better than the men and women who do this every day. And now look, she's gone and gotten herself killed." He had even tried to tell Ruth to go to the shelter, but she'd told him that she had a plan to help and that they'd thank her later for it.

Nate held Beth on his lap as his heart broke for her. Her mother had been the one that had died. Not his mate, but her mother. Not that it was any less horrific, but Beth was safe.

They had moved into their room when her body was discovered. He knew that something had happened…he had felt Beth's pain like his own…but he hadn't any idea that her mom had been killed until later, after they'd made sure Benton was dead.

He'd stood by Remy, who himself seemed a little dazed, as they looked at the dead woman that lay among the broken and bloodied trees. His mind had still been in battle mode, his sword out and slick with sweat. But he could only think of one thing. Ruth had died just as Beth had in his dreams.

She'd been torn in half and tossed away. Her broken body fragments had been far apart, her head and shoulders miles from her hips and legs. Remy had gathered the grisly scene up and taken her to the clinic. There was nothing they could do, of course, but leaving her out in the yard seemed cruel to everyone, and the faeries had even helped as much as they could. Nate had entered the room just as it was confirmed that it was Ruth Snow. Then Beth had come in and sat down on the floor. Picking her up, he'd brought her to their room, were she could talk and cry as needed.

"My dad, he's going to be...I'm not sure. Hurt for sure. And probably shocked." He said nothing, as he was sure that he wasn't required to point out that he might be a little relieved as well. "He had only just asked her for the divorce earlier today. She had told him...well, I'm sure you can imagine what she told him. Basically that he'd not be able to live without her there, and that he should get such thoughts out of his head. I can't believe that she's dead."

The faeries were going to make her a ring, something that Lyle or Beth could go to when they wanted, and Pitch had told him that it would be beautiful. He had no doubt that it would be. They loved Beth as much as Nate did.

And Benton was dead. It had seemed...well, it had seemed incredibly easy after all this time. Not only had they killed Benton by beheading him, but his body, something that they'd not thought of as going to be a problem, had disappeared as well. Remy said that he'd made arrangements with someone, but since he didn't elaborate, Nate didn't ask. Some things, he'd discovered of late, were better not knowing.

"My dad is going to be upset." Nate said nothing. He might be upset, but he might not care as much as he once might have. "I guess he will assuredly be staying here now; don't you think? Remy said he had a few jobs for him. My poor dad. He's not going to know what to do with himself. I know that it sounds terrible of me to say that, but I think he'll be a little glad that he won't have to deal with her anymore. I wonder how he'll be able to sell the house now. I mean, it's not like he can say that she was killed by a monster and tossed away like yesterday's leftovers." She giggled a little, and he knew that she was dealing the best way she could. She and her mom had been on the outs for some time, and this was hurting her deeper than she was letting on, he knew this. Nate could feel it.

"I've spoken to our computer wizard through the link we have. Jake is going to fix up some paperwork for him to take care of anything that he might need. There was an insurance policy on her and your dad that he was able to find. There will be a death certificate saying that she was killed in a car accident…much easier to explain, he said. That way your dad won't have to wait for seven years to have her declared dead. He'll be able to use the insurance money to get a fresh start." He wondered if he sounded cold, but Beth told him that her dad would like that. "Remy said he'd go and tell him. I didn't know if you wanted to be there or not."

"I do. I want to be there in case he needs me." Nate stood up with her in his arms and laid her on the bed. After crawling in with her, he was glad when she curled her body around his. "What happens now? I mean, you guys have spent a lot of time getting to this point. What are you going to do now?"

"I'm thinking you and I should find us a home in the city. Not too close to the others, but near enough that we can still get together. Chris and Kate are moving back here soon. They've already made arrangements to purchase two of the houses in one of the nicer neighborhoods, one for Rick and the other for Leo." She told him she'd like a nice little house. "I was thinking larger. For children."

She looked up at him. "Children? You mean the two of us having them?" He nodded and kissed her on the mouth. "There is a lot of work to be done yet, I thought. Rebuilding and such. Should we wait?"

"No. I don't want to wait, if you don't mind. I want to see new growth. You fat with a baby or two. I can go back to work at something...there are endless possibilities now that we're starting over. You can find work too. I guess your dad could use your help with his many projects." She rolled to her back and he looked down at her, resting his head on his hand as he continued. "I know you were like your father, an engineer, but I don't know what kind."

"Chemical. Dad is as well. And I taught math too, to high schoolers. How will we be able to afford this? I mean, even if I were to get a job, there are no banks and not much in the way of employers." He grinned at her. "You look like the cat who has only just discovered cream."

"The other realm, the one that Hector is from, the magic there continues to pay us even though the world is dead. I asked a while back about if the world were ever to be reinhabited, and he said that people had nothing to do with that magic. And even if the world were to crumble away, we'd not be hurt by that." He had even asked, quietly, about if Remy and Skylar went there and renewed the world, what would happen. Hector said nothing. They had done their job, and as far as the magic was concerned, they would continue to be paid as they had been forever. He told her about it. "It's enough money for us to live very well and never have to work again. But I'm not sure I can just sit around, especially after all of this."

"I want to work with my dad when it's time. But first I'd like to see the world. I mean, not just this country, but the entirety of it. All over the globe." He did as well. "Then I want to come back here, settle down with you, and have lots of babies."

He ran his hand down her shirt, using his claw to cut it away. When he had it torn from neck to hem, he leaned down and kissed the exposed part, nipping at her flesh as her breathing picked up. Pulling the pieces apart, he took her exposed breast into his mouth and suckled. Not hard, even though the thought of biting and feeding from her like this had him hard as rock. But when she held him to her, Nate removed all her clothing with just a thought, and looked down at the bounty that was all his.

"I love you with all that I am, Beth. I would like for you to marry me, if you would. Be my bride. Carry my children." He kissed her again, this time as gently as he could. "I love all that you are, and cannot imagine life without you. I don't even want to."

Moving down her body but sliding his between her legs, he wanted to eat her, fuck her, and do all sorts of things to her in between. Lifting her legs up so that they were on either side of his head, he blew gently over her heat and watched her face when she cried out.

"I love the way you don't hold back when I touch you." Her body laid back on the bed and he followed it. "I'm going to feast on you. Then if you give me what I want, I'm going to let my wolf have some of you. He so enjoyed that the other day."

"Yes, please. Both of you." Nate could smell her then, her need. And his wolf stirred along his body, seemingly begging for him to hurry so he could have his turn. Instead, he calmed him by saying that they had forever to be with her.

Nate licked her clit, then played with it using his tongue. Suckling it into his mouth, he slid his finger inside and fucked her while he ate her. Her juices trickled down his hand to the sheet under them as she rolled her hips up for more. Needing all of her, he buried his mouth over her and along with his fingers, fucked her with his tongue.

She tasted delicious. Her body rode his mouth, her fingers tugged then pulled his head down to her over and over. Every time he thought she was getting close, her body ready to fall over the edge, he would back off, nibble at her thighs, and tease her hips.

"Please, you're hurting me. I need to come." He didn't stop what he was doing, hurting himself by prolonging their lovemaking. "Nate, I'm going to murder you if you don't help me."

He smiled and let his wolf take him. Nate knew the exact moment when she realized he was no longer tasting her but his beast was. The wolf enjoyed her, letting her come several times while he ate her. Nate knew that his wolf's tongue was much different than his, so the wolf fucked her with long, thick strokes and drank deeply. When he licked her thigh where her pulse pounded, he didn't try to stop him when he bit her, marking his mate. He had a thought, wondering if all of his beasts would want to mark her, and figured they'd cross that bridge when they came to it. For now, he was having fun with his mate.

"Yes," she screamed at them both. Beth held him to her leg as she cried out several times that she was finished. Each time she came, his wolf tore a little deeper into her skin until she begged him to stop. With a small whimper, not only did he let her go, but he let Nate take him back as well. Nate licked the wound closed and noticed in the back of his mind that it was a perfect mark. The tats, it seemed, had made way for the scar that was there.

He moved up, taking small bites of her flesh and then sealing the wound with his tongue as he went. Beth came twice while he suckled at her breast. Two more times when he bit down on the hard tip and suckled from that. As he slid into her, no longer afraid of hurting her, he took her mouth and let her taste herself on his own.

"Come." She did, bowing up off the bed in a primal scream that made his balls tighten to his body. Even as he fucked her, the bed moved. Lifting her ass up, pounding her as deeply as he could go, he leaned into her throat and bit down just as his cock emptied.

Nate came twice more, his body seemingly having an endless supply of cum to fill her with. When she went limp under him, his own body nearly as spent, Nate sealed the wound he'd made and dropped on top of her. Rolling to his back took more energy than he thought he had, and he closed his eyes.

Just as he was letting sleep take him, he remembered the ring that he'd gotten made for her. He'd give it to her when they woke. Then perhaps they'd make love again.

~~~

Lyle stood over his wife's grave—a faerie ring, he reminded himself—and thought of all the things he wanted to say to her. Mostly his disappointment in her for getting herself killed, and upsetting Beth. He looked around and realized that he was alone, and wondered when it was everyone had left.

The ceremony had been perfect in all ways. Remy had said a few words, beautiful ones that he'd heard before, and had only just realized were very old. A poem that no one seemed to know the actual origins of, but touching nonetheless.

Do not stand at my grave and weep.
I am not there; I do not sleep.
I am a thousand winds that blow.
I am the diamond glints on snow.
I am the sunlight on ripened grain.
I am the gentle autumn rain.
When you awaken in the morning's hush
I am the swift uplifting rush
Of quiet birds in circled flight.
I am the soft stars that shine at night.
Do not stand at my grave and cry;
I am not there; I did not die.

Sitting on the pretty bench, he looked around the field where she'd been put to rest. It too had been just what he might have wanted for her. The faerie, Wooly, had told him that he would be able sit here no matter the weather and never be chilled or wet in the rain. The lady of the earth had told him so. He had wept at the kindness.

"They killed the monster, the one that murdered you." He tried to think how he felt about all this and couldn't. Things were just too...fresh, he supposed. "I came up with a serum that took away his strength that made it possible. Weston, the doctor here, he thinks he'll be able to use the reverse formula to do great things with it. I don't know what yet, but I'm going to work with him for as long as he'll allow it. So will our Beth. She deserves this chance to be something after what you did to her."

Weston had told him forever. And it wasn't until he talked

with Remy, a good man too, that he'd found out that because he had been invited to help them, he got the same benefits the rest of them had. Immortality.

"They've decided to use the motor homes as sort of a traveling medical unit for a while. Hard to say how many people are out there, sick or hurt, that were too afraid to come out until now. Some of the faeries, they're painting them now. There'll be a big colorful cross on the side of them. They said that they would bring cheer to those in need. I think they're right. And I also think you would have hated it." He thought of the few people that had come in after the monster was down, how badly they'd been starved and in need of help, both mentally and physically. "I'm going to stay here too, with Beth and Nate. They're talking of getting a house big enough for me to live with them. I don't know if I will, but they invited me and I told her I'd think on it."

One of the faeries that had befriended him, Woolly, came to sit with him. The man was old, he'd told him, centuries older than even he was. And at times like this, Lyle was feeling his age and more. But the little man had been both a comfort and joy to him. He thought he'd see if he wanted to come and stay with him when he found where he was going to rest his head.

"You tell her about your day?" He said that he'd been telling her about things. "You go on now, tell her everything. You should be proud of what you've done for us magic folks. The sheep and cows, they never had it so good. All on account of you."

"I didn't do anything but get Remy to buy the ranch out there. It was a good investment for all of them." Woolly said he could go on thinking that, but he thought it was right fine of him. "The tea that you're going to use, you know that we'll still need to work on it. Get the right mixture of water and poop."

"Yeah, I'm getting that worked out. We got some test plots, just like you told us. I'm thinking that we're going to have more blooms than we've ever had before after we put some of it on the flower gardens. And Ann is as happy as a lark, she is, with that herb place you had put in. Got her a whole crew of brownies working the weeds and rocks out as we speak." Lyle nodded and looked down at the ring of flowers again. "I heard tell that anyone in their own faerie ring can hear being talked to. If you don't mind me saying, I'm thinking that's the only way you're gonna get a word in sideways with your dearly departed. She sure could talk a lot."

Lyle smiled. He could have taken offense, he supposed, but what would have been the point in that? The man was right. When he flew up to look him in the eye, Lyle let him have a gander, as the man called it. When he seemed satisfied, he told him he'd be around if he needed him, but not to forget about the other stuff. Then he was alone again.

Lyle enjoyed the quiet a great deal, but he thought that it wouldn't last long. He knew that he'd need to have someone to talk to, even if it was just to ask a question or two of. Lyle had even been given a dog of his very own, his first since he'd been married. One of the strays that had wandered in one day had taken a liking to him.

"Woolly and I are working on some projects together; he wanted me to tell you about them. He's adopted me as his go to human, he said. Anyway, we're going to see about making a tea, a fertilizer for the flowers that can be used and not harm the earth. Did you know that they make the new faeries by the queen kissing the blossoms in the spring?" He felt silly telling her that, and looked out beyond the trees again. "I would guess your answer to that would be poppycock, something you were very fond of saying when things were not up to your way of thinking. I've no doubt that you'd have plenty to say about a great many things going on right now."

Lyle could see them there, the little people working. All his life he'd thought when he'd looked out, as he was now, that he was seeing flies or some other kind of bug. But it had been these people, working to keep the earth as clean and happy as they could, while humans and paranormals alike kept killing it.

"In a few weeks there is going to be a wedding. Beth is marrying Nate too, but all the people here, all the ones that came together to make this world a better place, are going to be wed in a huge ceremony. It's going to be some kind of party, I think." He smiled when he thought of Beth, his baby girl, getting married. "She's asked me to give her away. It's not going to be your regular kind of wedding, there won't be much in the way of humans there, but it will be beautiful. And Nate, he's got my little girl a big surprise lined up as a gift. He's taking her on a long cruise to see the world."

They'd be gone a whole two months, and he was gonna stay here in the big house to help Weston with some things and keep an eye on the flowers while they were gone. Not that the others living there wouldn't be around as well, but he was going to help the little people out by being the big guy. And he was going to oversee the gardens around the house too. It was going to be a big undertaking, as it had been neglected for a long time. He thought of his wife of nearly forty years, and decided that he had a few things to tell her.

"You weren't a nice person, Ruth. The longer I've been thinking on it, the more I come to realize that you never were. At first you were all right, a little pushy, but I could always escape to work when you got to be too much. Then when I retired, I got to where I didn't like being around you even for a minute. I never thought about it before, but you drove Beth away with your constant harping on her. And she told me what you did with her first employer. How could you do that to someone you're supposed to love? I just...I guess I shouldn't have been surprised, but Ruth, that was just terrible of you. I don't think you had anything to do with her heart problems, but had she lived at home like you tried to make her, I don't think she would have made it here to young Nate. And that would be a shame. Never seen a couple so in love before." His guilt for talking this way to his dead wife was waning, and he was getting stronger for it. "You never would have approved of anything that they're doing, would you? You would have pushed and shoved all her ideas for her big day aside and done things your way. If you had let them wed at all. She would have been hurt by it, but she'd have done it just to keep the peace. Which is something that rarely worked out with you, but we did try."

He felt horrible for being so honest with her at this point, but Lyle knew that he needed to get some things off his chest. He'd been under her thumb for a very long time, and he needed this as much as anyone did.

"I loved you, Ruth. Loved you with all my heart when I first met you. You were vibrant, funny. You would have helped anyone that needed you. Then after Beth was born, you became so controlling, but I felt once she was older you'd back off. I thought for sure you were just going through a phase and would get over it when she went to school that first time. Kindergarten was so exciting for Beth, and even that you had to have some rule over. But you never did back off, did you? I never told you this before, but the school called me one day. Asked me to have you step down as room mom. Said that the children didn't like you and that the other moms were hurt when you were always making them do things your way. Even other kids' birthday parties had to be approved by you or you'd mess it up. What kind of woman does that to kids?" The trees began to sway a little, and he realized that it was getting dark. In a few weeks it would be spring and the days would be getting much longer. "I'm gonna change the subject now, Ruth. You know what you did, and there isn't any point in rehashing it now."

His heart pained him a bit. Telling his dead wife what a horrible person she'd been was making him feel slightly better about not missing her now that she was gone. But he was sure that if Woolly was right and she could hear him, she was pissed off now.

"There's a meeting soon that is going to tell us about what Remy and Skylar are going to do. I guess there is some talk about them going away, to this other place and making it right. No one knows for sure if they'll go or not. Or what might happen when they get there. I don't know a great deal about what all these beings can do, but they sure are strong. Magic." He laughed a little. "Me, a man of science, believing in magic. I guess not everything can be explained away because of science, huh?"

"Your lordship?" He looked at the little person who was near the ring of flowers. When she bowed before him, he wanted to turn and look to see who deserved such a title, and knew it was him. No matter how many times he said he was just plain Lyle Snow, they continued to call him lordship. "Do you have a moment?"

"I have all the time in the world. What do you need?" He watched her pace back and forth on the stones that were just around the flowers there; whatever it was, he'd not interrupt her thinking process. Faeries were not to be rushed, no matter what. And they didn't want you to talk to them either. Thinking, apparently, had rules.

"The lady of the water, she has released the lake again." He wasn't sure what that meant, but waited for her to explain. "Oh, I'm sorry...I'm Buff. Anyway, the lady of the water has released the lake, and we're to fill it. I'm not sure what that means other than to put a few fish in it and tell them to breed. We can even help them with that, but we try to stay out of such matters."

"Probably should be left to those who know." She smiled at him, then frowned. "Perhaps if you let me know what the issue is, I can help you work it out."

"There is an elixir. A magical potion that is to be put in the water when it is filled to capacity. It's magical, you see. And once it's in the water, all things that drink from it, or even use it for bathing...well, they'll have good health and the ability to be fertile." He nodded. That made sense, he supposed. To help populate the earth, there would be times when help would be needed. "They drank it."

He had to think what she'd been saying. There was nothing there, nothing she'd said so far that cleared it up, so he asked her. "Who drank it? And what will happen to them now that they have?"

"Babies. Lots of babies." He nodded. Again, this made perfect sense to him, but he still hadn't gotten to the root of it just yet. "They'll have more than one at a time for a little while too. Even after the first birthing, they'll have many children and be ripe sooner as well."

"Well, that'll certainly do the trick in getting more... what are we talking about? Faeries?" She explained to him that faeries had no children, and that the queen helped create them. "Oh, I see. So whoever drank this, they're going to have lots of babies in a little while. How long?"

"The usual time." She came to sit on his knee and paced again. "I'm not sure what to tell the queen. She told me to keep the magic close to me, but I had to run a very quick errand, and when I returned it was gone. It took me forever to find the bottle that it had been in. You should have seen it, your lordship. When the magic was shaken up in it, the colors were akin to a rainbow after a pretty storm. The glass itself was made of the most beautiful shades of emerald that we could find. Then it was spun together in such a way that only a few could see its worth. I'm sure that they meant no harm in drinking it."

"And these people who drank it…do you suppose they'll be upset when they find out what they've done? I mean, to the point of coming here and removing a few heads?" She stared at him with wide eyes. "Are these people someone that I can talk to? I'll do my best to save you, young Buff. But you have to tell me who they are."

"The women of the brotherhood, your lordship. I thought I had told you." He shook his head as what she'd just told him started to come together. "They will all be fertile now that they have it in their systems, and when they are mated with their males, a child—well, children—will be created right away. They will all be breeding at the same time, for they all enjoyed several glasses of it."

"Several glasses? I thought you said it was a vase created by your kind." She nodded. "Then it's not wee little, but big."

"Nay, not too big, but it is endless in its supply. As I said, they consumed several glasses of it." Lyle smiled. "Do you think them to be upset enough with me that they should remove my head? I would not like that at all. Not one bit, I think."

"No. And if anyone gets upset, you.... They're going to *all* have babies?" She nodded again and smiled. "Holy shit, I'm going to be a grandda."

Lyle sat there for several seconds, his mind trilling around at the thought of being a grandda, and got up and did a little dance. Grandda. He was going to be the best damned one in the world. And his little baby was going to be a momma. This was cause for a celebration. Lyle was still dancing around as he made his way to the house. One thought kept going through his mind; Beth and Nate would be the best parents.

Chapter 11

Skylar and the others were all in the room with her, and Beth was beginning to feel slightly closed in. Going to the window to try and catch her breath, Jamey sat down beside her and pulled open the window. Beth had a feeling that the window hadn't had that ability before, but said nothing. She was just grateful for the fresh breeze. And like a great many other things in this building, it was beginning to not bother her as much as it had.

"This is going to be epic, don't you think?" Beth nodded. It was going to be beautiful too. "I'm so excited that I'm about to wet myself."

They both laughed and looked around the room, and at the women there. Where they had gotten the dresses that each of them wore was something she'd only given a little thought to, but they had chosen well. All of them wore something that said a lot about the woman. And each of them looked as beautiful as the other. Beth felt pretty herself.

Skylar's dress was long, full, and seemingly a traditional gown. But it wasn't, not really. It was decorated, not by pearls or beads, but with flowers. Each flower on the dress had been put there by magic, and the design was simply breathtaking. The faeries had each brought her one and had put it to the cloth in honor of her status as Remy's bride. The color wasn't garish or gaudy, but it made her look like she'd stepped from a faerie tale and had a story to tell. It was perfect for the beautiful woman.

Vicki's dress was the only one that wasn't white. Hers was a blood red that seemed to shimmer when she moved. Even her veil of the same color looked to sparkle off even the smallest of light, and suited the woman a great deal. She seemed to shine with happiness.

Jamey's dress was white, but the decorations along the hem and train at the back were dragons, each of them in different colors that seemed to come alive when she walked. Beth was a little envious of the woman...she was so strong and brave, and could be something as spectacular as a dragon. What person wouldn't like to change into that?

Kate's dress was beautiful in a simple way. A short dress with a long train that dragged the floor, it was covered in small dark panthers. Each one of them was made of flowers, their scent giving the headiest aroma that made anyone near her smile.

But it was Ryiah's dress that made them all pale in comparison. The faeries had come to help her dress. And when the woman had put on a plain white shift, Kate had been slightly disappointed. But just after they were told they had twenty minutes before it was time for the wedding to begin, the room filled with faeries of every color and they attached themselves to her in some way. Her living dress made her look like the faerie princess that she was. And a dozen of the male faeries had put on her veil and were going to carry it down the aisle when it was time for her to be wed to Rick.

"You do know that you're as gorgeous as the rest of us, don't you?" Beth looked over at Jamey when she spoke. "When they said that Woolly and your dad were going to design your dress, I thought you'd be upset. I think I might have been. But Christ almighty, woman, they made you shine. I don't think I've ever seen a dress more suited to someone than this is you."

She looked down at the creation that her dad had presented her with. He'd worked all night on it, he'd told her, and she could tell. The dress and all its beauty was a one of a kind work of art. And she had both men to thank for it.

Handprints. There were millions of handprints all over her dress. And with each print, a name had been added of the one who had put it there. She only had to look at the dress and see a different name, a new set of hands. And each of them had used the color of their wings. She touched one of the names that had no prints, but meant a great deal to the people who had asked for it to be there. It simply said *Hunter*.

"Hunter was an amazing person. I wish you could have met her. And she loved Ryiah like they were sisters." Beth had heard that too, from anyone who saw her name there. "When she was murdered, it took Ryiah a long time to get over it. I'm not even sure that she has fully. Hunter saved her life and the others that were there that day."

"Whey told me that there is a ring for her in the gardens. I haven't been to see it yet, but I plan to go when we get back. The queen said that they would miss her forever. I believe her. Everyone has told me of all the things she did. And how she came to be. Such a tragic and wonderful love story." Jamey nodded and looked away. The tears that seemed to be there all the time threatened to fall again, and she had to look away herself.

Beth put her hand on her belly and thought of the children that were there. Twins. She was going to have twins in less than nine months, and she and Nate were as excited as they could be. Already they were making decisions for the things they'd need when they arrived. There was an endless list of things out there for newborns, all the way up until they were adults. Too many for her and Nate to decide on right now, but they would. And her dad had finally agreed to come and live with them when they figured out where that might be. She looked around the room again.

They were all breeding, as Nate had called it. All of them were also having multiple births, too, all of them twins... except, of course, Skylar, who was having triplets. Beth still thought that the magic that they'd all drank that day had been set out on purpose. They'd been in the living room when one of them said they needed a drink, and had found the bottle on the counter with condensation on it and six glasses around it. But it was the best trick anyone could have played on her. She thought the others were happy as well.

The music sounded and she stood up with the rest of them. Her dad came into the room; a man of honor, they'd called him, as he was giving them all away. His ever present friend, Wooly, was at his shoulder, his little tux as gorgeous as her father's. And the flowers at both their lapels were perfectly matched too.

Her dad had blossomed over the last few weeks, and finding out about the babies had given him a nice pep in his step. Beth knew that he talked to her mom every day. And when he did, he came back saddened but looking stronger. She was sure that this had been the only time in his life he'd been free to say what he wanted. Dad kissed each one of them and stood in the middle of the six brides, three on either side of him.

"A man could die happy with a thing like this to keep him warm on a cold winter night." She kissed him on the cheek and wiped away the tears she tasted there. "I've never told you this before, or if I have, it's still as true now as it was before. I've been more proud to be your father than any man in the world could be. And I'm happy that you're going to have a man in your life that I not only respect, but think of as my son already. I love you, Bethy. With all my heart."

"And I love you, Daddy. Thank you for being the best pop in the world, and I know that you're going to be the greatest pop-pop our children could ever know too."

As they made their way out into the bright sunshine, Beth thought of all the changes in her life over the last few weeks. She no longer had a heart problem, she'd met the man of her dreams, her father was happy, and she was a part of a group that made the world spin. And on top of that, she was going to be a mom. Life was good.

~~~

Nate tugged at his collar again. It wasn't tight, not after a little zap of magic from Rick, but he still felt strangled by it. The rest of them, all the men, looked equally uncomfortable, except for Remy. And the man looked as if he'd been born to wear a tux. Christ, it fit him like a glove, and even though the man was at least a fifty-six long because of all the massive muscle he had, he looked good. Not that Nate's was any smaller; he'd been measured to a sixty long. He'd not even been sure that was a size until then.

At seven four he could carry his weight well, he supposed, but he still felt like he'd been stuffed in a taco and sour cream had been spread all over him. He did not wear suits. Rick came to stand behind him and grinned.

"You do know that once Beth sees you, you're going to realize how much all this is worth it, don't you?" Nate said he wasn't so sure. "Trust me. She's going to be all over you. Like

175

I'm hoping my own bride will be when we're done here."

Looking in the mirror to make sure that he'd not messed up his tie again, he thought of his wife to be. They were going to be parents. And just after the New Year. What a way to start fresh, he thought. A family.

By this time tomorrow they'd be on a ship headed for France. He'd never been there himself, but was looking forward to it as much as Beth. And thanks to Rick, a man not without resources, he told them, they were going to hop from one of his homes to the next over the next eight weeks until they were back in the States and ready to settle down. He had also landed him a job, one that he was looking forward to.

"You ready?" He nodded to Remy when he asked. "I'm truly glad that they insisted we do this. I'm really glad to have her as my true wife. I think Skylar would have lived with me forever without the paperwork to say we were wed, but I think this is proper."

"Have you made a decision on the other?" He looked at him, then away. "You're going to do it, aren't you? You're going to go there and bring that world back to life."

"I'm not positive, but I think we have to. Don't you?" Nate said he wasn't sure he could do it. "I know what everyone has said, they'd miss us. But Ryiah, she assures me that we can all go back and forth through the doorways and visit here as well. Not for as long, but we can come for things. And bring the babes with us. To think after all this time I'm to be a father of triplets. I cannot wait, but will admit I'm a little nervous as well."

"So am I. I don't remember ever even holding someone else's baby, much less my own. I mean, my stepbrother had children and I was there when they were little, but I never held them. They're so tiny. And we're not exactly what I'd call normal sized men." Remy laughed when he did. "It's a lot to get used to, don't you think?"

"Aye, it is. But we'll do fine with it. It'll come as natural as anything." Nate nodded. "You and Beth, you're good people. I'm glad to call you friends."

Nate hugged the older man. It had been a long time, a very long time, since he'd wanted that contact with another man. But Remy was indeed his friend, more than likely one that he would call that for the rest of his days. Rembrandt was a good man, and there were very few of them left in this world.

They were standing together in front of the large flower-decorated trellis when the doors to the compound opened a few minutes later. Nate's breath caught when he saw his Beth, and he wanted to rush to her and grab her up in his arms. Remy's softly spoken, "Steady man," was the only thing that kept him still.

"They be like springtime; don't you think?" He agreed with the man and felt his love for Beth soar higher. He glanced at the other women and thought his bride the most beautiful of them all. But then, he could have been slightly prejudiced about that.

The ceremony was over in a matter of minutes. The clergy had said that he'd make it group vows, and that he'd only single them out when he blessed their union and when he introduced them to the crowd. Nate wondered what the man thought of the crowd that was there, but figured that someone would have thought of him being human and all of them, in some way, had maybe tweaked the man's vision so he only saw what he needed to.

"I love you." Nate took his new wife in his arms when she spoke to him. "I cannot wait for us to be alone."

"Me either. But I think we can arrange something a little private. If you promise to be quiet." She told him she wasn't making any promises. "Well, I can live with that too."

Picking her up in his arms, he took them to the sky. He wasn't too bad at the landing or taking off part yet, but he did have a little trouble steering. Nate was going to work on that soon. But for now, he was going to enjoy himself.

Taking her to the nearest tree at the top of the mountain, he pressed her against it as he kissed her. She was naked beneath his hands when he touched her, and he looked down at her tight belly. Their children grew there. Nate dropped to his knees to reach out to them, feeling their small heartbeats as if they were his own. Putting his hands on her, he kissed her flesh and wondered what they would be.

"Happy." He looked up at Beth when she spoke. "I don't care what they are, girl, boy, shifter, or human, I just want to make sure that they're happy. Forever."

"As do I." Kissing his children again, he made his way downward to the apex of Beth's thighs. Holding her in his hand, he pulled her closer to him and tasted her. She was wet already, and he could smell her scent...a new one now that she was breeding. "I love the way you are soaking wet for me. I could easily drink from you for hours and not get enough."

Lifting one of her legs up so that it rested on his shoulder, he buried his mouth over her and began to feast. And what a feast it was.

She not only rode his mouth as he drank from her, but when he slid his fingers into her, fucking her with them, she soaked his hand as well. And when she pulled him back from her, he nearly growled when she told him it was her turn. Standing and turning to the tree like she said to, Nate fisted his cock as he waited for her to take him.

"I love it when you come on me." He nodded, nearly pulling his dick off when she slid her fingers into her pussy and then took the wet digits to her mouth. "You have no idea how sexy I find it when you taste like me after you eat me. The way we taste together, our juices. I could come after that."

"Christ, baby, you're killing me." He wanted her to take him, but he loved watching her play too. "Feed me your breasts. I want to suck them hard enough that they bruise for me."

"No, I'm in charge right now." He nodded, not sure that he could take much more. "Stop touching yourself. That is mine."

He nearly fell back when she dropped in front of him and took him in her hands. He wasn't sure what to expect from her, this new confident person, but when she kissed the tip of his cock, Nate had a feeling that he was going to be in deep shit before this was over. And the moment that she swirled her tongue around his crown, he knew a whole new level of need.

She sucked his balls into her mouth, cupped them in her palms. When she gave them a slightly rough twist, Nate felt his knees tremble and his balls tighten to his body. Every time she moved over him, took him in her mouth, licked the thick pulsing vein down his shaft, he hurt. And he knew that when he came, which was beginning to look like never, he was going to hurt with that as well.

He was sweating and chilled at the same time. His body went from feeling like he was on the verge of a heart attack to the most powerful pain he'd ever experienced. Just when he was ready to take her, she leaned back on her knees and opened her mouth.

Grabbing his cock in his hands, he held his balls tight.

They hurt, he wasn't kidding, but the thought of releasing on her was making his hands move faster. The cum that dripped off the tip of him, mixed with her saliva, made the slide quick and smooth. And when he felt it, his body erupt, he watched her as every drop hit her beautiful body.

"Again, Nate. I need more."

He didn't stop jerking off over her. Every time he thought he was finished, she would beg him for more. When finally he could give her nothing else, she laid back on the branch and rubbed his juices all over her. Nate joined her…it was her turn to feed him.

Her pussy was so wet that his cock slid into her effortlessly. As he made love to her slowly, not sure that he could do much more than that, he touched her. His hands molded her to his body, his legs wrapped her tighter to him. And when she cried out that she was coming, for him to come with her, he felt his balls fill again and he emptied into her, marveling at the power her commands had over him. Nate dropped then, his body not spent so much as drained. He was finished.

When he woke he was on his back, her spread over him, and he knew that it had only been a few moments. The birds were still gone from their perches and his heart was still a little erratic. Smiling at what a sight they must make, he held her tightly to him when he saw the deer come out of the woods to feed.

It had been a long while since he'd seen much in the way of wildlife. Months and months since he'd seen a squirrel, or even a fly. But as he lay there resting, he saw all sorts of creatures venturing out. As he watched, two doe came out to join the buck, along with three small fawns who weren't old enough to even have shed their spots.

Nate had come from the city. He'd grown up riding his

bike to his friends' houses, marveling at how much food they seemed to have in their homes all the time, and envying them their seemingly loving family. Nate had had a good life other than it being very poor and cold, just not much of it had been spent anywhere that there were wild animals. The first time he'd shifted, he'd been so afraid that he'd —

"Do you suppose anyone has missed us?" Letting go of the memory with ease, he told Beth that he doubted any of the newlyweds had hung around much after they left. "I guess. But we have to go back and have some cake. I've been looking forward to it all day."

She stretched over him and he felt his cock stir. When she stood up and was dressed, Nate didn't know if he was disappointed or relieved. He wasn't sure how much more he had in him if she wanted him again. But like a good soldier, he'd do his best, he thought with a smile.

"Your dad has all his things moved into the building from the motor home. I think he's relieved to not have to use it any more. I think he's looking forward to being caretaker a little too much. Do you suppose he and Woolly will be getting into trouble?" Beth said she hoped so. "Yeah, I guess I do too."

He stood up and dressed himself. Nate did put his tux back on, but didn't bother with the tie. As far as he was concerned, he was finished with them for the rest of his long life.

Nate noticed that not only was Rick and Ryiah missing when they returned, but Leo and Jamey had disappeared as well. Smiling, he accepted a piece of the cake and sat at one of the many picnic tables that had been set up. Instead of eating though, he looked around at the people.

Most of them were from the other realm. There were a few humans here, people that had come to get food and shelter when things were at their worst. He noticed, too, that a great many people had faeries hitching a ride on some part of their body. Mostly shoulders, but a few had them on their hair. He wondered what they would do now. Where would they go?

When Remy sat next to him, his hair mussed and his tie at half mast, Nate smiled at his plate. There were at least four pieces of cake on it, as well as a bowl of fruit. The man ate almost as much as he did.

"You have things finished that you needed to be done? I mean with the paperwork on Ruth, it's all squared away then?" Nate told him that as far as he knew things were complete. "Good, good. Lyle has helped us figure out the gas pumps, so we can use those now. The electrical plant is up and running as well, so there will be homes with power all over." Remy ate two pieces of the cake before he continued. "He's being paid. Not sure yet how much he's getting, but he told me a bit ago that he'd gotten a lot of jewels and gold with cash delivered this morn. I think he thought he'd been set up for a robbery."

"He told me about it. I think he was a little freaked out about it at first. But he said that he's going to invest in the town. I think he means to try and teach a little too. Not the kids, but some of the people here." Remy nodded. He was slightly distracted, Nate knew that. "I suppose you could just tell me or ask me and stop beating around the bush so much."

Remy grinned. "We're going to the new realm tomorrow. We've decided that we can do more good there than becoming fat and lazy here. I talked with Ryiah. I didn't want to harm the babies with this type of work, and she said that because of their purity that they'd add to the magic rather than be harmed by it." Nate was going to miss the big man and Skylar, and told him that. "Skylar wants to make sure that we come together at some point soon. She has it in her head that now that we're finished, we'll scatter. She might be right. It's been a lot over the last year or so for you all."

"Yes, but you've been dealing with this the longest. And you seem to have your head on right." He nodded, but looked sad. "Who are you taking with you? I'm assuming that you will. One of us?"

"Aye, we've talked it over. We were thinking you and Beth. Her dad will stay here; he's needed much more than any of the rest of us now that we can move about. Beth has some intelligence and experience that we might need there at some point. And you...well, I need you." He asked him why. "You are my friend. Even though you didn't want to be here—and to be honest, we thought you'd not make it when you first arrived—I've watched you grow and become a good man. A man that I would call my best friend."

Nate was honored and overwhelmed at the same time. He couldn't speak around the emotions, and nodded twice before he had to look away. Tears filled his eyes, and he wasn't sure what to do about them other than to let them fall.

"I'd have to talk to Beth." Remy said he understood that. Nate turned to him then and saw that he wasn't immune to the emotions either. "You don't know what this means to me. Even if we can't do this for some reason, you have given me more in this one thing than I can ever explain to you."

"As has your friendship to me. As I said, you have become a good friend. And it is I who am honored to have gotten to know you." When he put out his hand, Nate took it. It was more than a handshake to him, it was a bond that only two men could make.

183

Chapter 12

Beth felt her heart break for the devastation of the other realm. There was nothing here. No trees that lived, no people to tend the dead gardens. Even the smell, the odor of death and other things that she had no name for, seemed to linger in the air as if it had no place to go. She saw the woman in the distance coming toward them, and knew that she was the Keeper…this world's version of Kate. Adaline would not be able to leave with them when this magic came to pass.

"I've been told you were coming today. Not a wonderful time here, but we can fix that right up. I'm happy to meet you." She shook all their hands and then hugged her and Skylar. "Babes. You bring new life here, not only in the form of the earth, but in real life as well. I'm so happy to meet you all."

"Ryiah said that you'd know what we had to do." Adaline told Remy that she'd been given instructions. Pulling out the paper, she looked around before reading it. Remy continued when he looked at the devastation as well. "'Tis bad, is it not? And very unnecessary. Those men, they hurt not just the people here, but all living creatures. It's a sad shame that it's come to this.

"I think so as well. But was needed, I think, too. To start fresh, not many beings get to do that. Some should, but few get the chance." Adaline looked at them then. "You should know that the doorways have been set up. Hector helped me on your end, but there are four doorways ready to be set here when you have things finished. I've set them aside in my home so that they'll be ready when you come back. You'll go back to your home while the land works. The other realm will need you for a bit when the place here is coming to life."

"Yes. Ryiah said that we'd be in the way here for a time. She said that you'd not be able come with us. That you have to stay and record things that happen. I'm sorry for that." She only smiled at her. "How long have you been here?"

"Forever." Adaline smiled at her then. "It's hard to imagine, is it not, that someone would be in a place that has no beginning and no end? That is what we have here. Not a new beginning, but a fresh one. One that I think, with your help, will be better than ever before. And will go on being some place that people will want to live and work. You are going to be good leaders and guides here in this new realm. It is an honor for me to be even a small part of it with you."

"I don't know how you managed it. Especially in the last few months." Adaline told Skylar that she had had her books. "What do we need to do first?"

"You know the words you're to say?" Remy and Skylar nodded. "Good. That'll be the first thing. Once you say them, you'll stand back to back, then your marks will touch. Then we just wait. I don't know how long, but that's all you do."

Remy and Skylar both got to their knees and took a handful of the dry dirt into their hand. Adaline handed them both a cup of water, and Beth and Nate held the seeds that had been plucked from two of the plants that Hector had brought to the world not long ago.

"We devote all that we are to this realm. Give it our blood

when it is necessary at war, our tears when we have joy. We will celebrate this new beginning by coming here freely and without qualms. The four of us together will give this land rebirth and hopefully new life." Remy cut into his palm, and then Skylar did the same.

Beth and Nate weren't required to do so, but had said that they would. This was going to be their world as well, and they wanted to be as much a part of it as they could. All four of them let their blood drip into the earth. When they were finished with that, the seeds were planted in the dirt, the water poured over it in hopes the roots would catch. When they stood up, Beth moved back, none of them sure what was going to happen.

When they were back to back, Skylar and Remy locking their arms together, Beth lifted their shirts up so that they could be skin to skin. They were as ready as they'd ever be. After sitting down on the earth next to Nate, he took her hand in his and kissed it.

"I'm glad that we're getting to witness this. And be here." He kissed her again. "I love you, Nate. Very much."

"And I love you."

He looked around when she did. The ground beneath them began to shake a little, and they both stood up. Remy and Skylar were still together, and Beth went to them when Nate did. Wrapping her arms around the two of them, Nate did the same, and they watched the movement as the four of them huddled together as if they were protecting each other. Beth hoped that it wouldn't come to that.

At first it was small things. The earth seemed to settle somehow. Trees toppled over, and whatever buildings were standing near them began to fall as well. When the area was level — well, as level as it could be — Beth could see far out and knew that this was the start.

Debris from the houses that had been here began to disappear; broken and splintered, when they were sucked down into the soil, it was quick. Trees, all them dried out and dead, were brought down as well. Soon there was nothing left except dark dirt. But she knew that this was only the beginning.

Nothing else happened for several minutes. But then the seeds they planted began to sprout up. That was when they noticed that all across the land, other things began to move the ground to come up for the sun. When the seedlings were high and full of green, Adaline told them it was time for them to go. Time for them to let the ground do what it needed.

As they stepped into the opening of the machine that would be the only thing left on this realm that was from before, Beth looked out again. It had started…all the earth here was greening up, and she could see small life in the soil.

Water began to fill the valleys that were being formed. Trees were growing at a fast pace. As the doors closed, she saw grass growing and rocks pushing up from the earth.

This new world was going to be wonderful.

Before You Go...

HELP AN AUTHOR

write a review

THANK YOU!

Share your voice and help guide other readers to these wonderful books. Even if it's only a line or two your reviews help readers discover the author's books so they can continue creating stories that you'll love. Login to your favorite retailer and leave a review. Thank you.

Kathi Barton, author of the bestselling series Force of Nature, lives in Nashport, Ohio with her husband Paul. In addition to writing full time Kathi likes to spend time with her eight grandkids, three children and three children-in-laws. She writes to relax and have fun.

Her muse, a cross between Jimmy Stewart and Hugh Jackman brings them to life for her readers in a way that has them coming back time and again for more. Her favorite genre is paranormal romance with a great deal of spice. You can visit Kathi on line and drop her an email if you'd like. She loves hearing from her fans. aaronskiss@gmail.com.

Follow Kathi on her blog: http://kathisbartonauthor.blogspot.com/

Nathaniel

Nathaniel

Nathaniel

Nathaniel

Nathaniel

Nathaniel

Nathaniel

Nathaniel

Nathaniel

Nathaniel

Nathaniel

Nathaniel

Nathaniel

Nathaniel

Nathaniel

Nathaniel

Nathaniel

www.ingramcontent.com/pod-product-compliance
Lightning Source LLC
Chambersburg PA
CBHW032117170626
46808CB00006B/1981